THE IMPROBABLE RISE
OF PACO JONES

Dominic Carrillo

CSP Publishing

The Improbable Rise of Paco Jones

CSP
CreateSpace
Independent Publishing

ACKNOWLEDGMENTS

Thank you to all the students I have ever taught. You have given me the inspiration and insight for this story. Thanks to John O'Brien for designing the cover. Thank you to Tricia Quinn, Tania Carrillo, Azul Terronez, Rebecca Battistoni, and Amy Mortenson for your critical feedback. And a huge thanks to Jennifer Redmond Silva for her excellent professional editing work, feedback and guidance.

DEDICATION

To the bicultural or biracial kids out there who have gone through the pain and confusion—along with the curiosity and beauty—of navigating the world and their identities without ever fitting neatly into one category.

And to my parents, who had the love and courage to make a bicultural family when others disapproved.

PROLOGUE

13+13= 26.

My age.

As an 8th grade English teacher, that makes me relatively old—to them. Twice their age.

The 13's are two students sitting in the front row, ten minutes early for my next class.

I sit at my desk behind a computer and remember glimpses of my 13-year-old self.

Sure, I said and did some dumb things back then. But I was also a thoughtful and conscious being, much like the students in my classes—though they don't seem to get much credit for it. Instead, they're dismissed by many adults as Internet-iPhone-video-game-zombies. The truth is that there's a lot going on behind the scenes, in their heads and under their skin.

I see it everyday.

I hear it when they don't think I'm listening.

Like right now. These two don't realize that I am paying attention. *What are they doing?* Watching the trailer to the next James Bond film on YouTube. *What are they saying?*

"Those skeleton masks are awesome, man."

"That's Dia de los Muertos in Mexico."

"I wanna' do that for Halloween. That's cool."

A far cry from when I was in junior high.

They used to *call me* things like "Dia De Los Muertos" and "Taco Jones," and it was far from "cool."

Now I am the teacher and they call me Mr. Jones—kind of weird. Most of my students don't know that my first name is Paco, and none have any idea what happened to me when I was their age. They probably can't even imagine me as a middle schooler.

But I can.

I remember the 8th grade—and Naomi, Trent, Tequila, and 'The Game'—like it was yesterday.

TACOS AND POOP

I was almost done with my first semester of 8th grade at Walden Academy.

I sat outside, alone on a bench in the middle of lunch recess on that cloudy, mild California day.

A group of seven friends—the "cool kids"—were sitting at the table they'd claimed way back on the first day of school. It was an exclusive club. Nobody else dared sit there. Five 8th grade boys sat with two pretty girls and they laughed hysterically at themselves and the objects of their ridicule. The mighty Trent Oden was their leader. They all wore designer sweatshirts and two-hundred-dollar custom-made Nikes. With mandatory plain uniforms, this was how Walden kids distinguished themselves: their shoes. The footwear at their table alone must have amounted to more than 1,000 bucks.

I looked down at my feet. The collective value of the shoes at my one-man lunch party: $19.99.

As I opened my lunch bag I saw something else I'd never noticed before: My skin was almost as brown as my bag.

Damn!

I'd never thought about my skin color at my old school, Dolores.

So I was isolated, and more or less a loser that day—actually, that entire semester. I poked open my juice box, pulled out three foil-wrapped tacos and some salsa my mom had packed, and started eating.

When the group of so-called cool kids quieted down it got my attention. They were usually loud and obnoxious. So I looked up from my tacos and made eye contact with their table.

That's when they started laughing at me.

Maybe they'd made fun of my Payless shoes that looked like bootleg imitations. Or maybe it was my plain blue sweatshirt, cheap and label-less. Maybe there was food on my face, or my hair was all messed up? I looked over my shoulder to make sure a circus clown wasn't standing directly behind me.

Then a boy named Paul pointed at me and shouted, "Viva los Tacos! Whoo!"

Everyone at their table started laughing hysterically.

This confused me.

I didn't see the humor in my tacos or my appearance.

Then I heard: "Holy crap, Paco's eating frickin' tacos!"

I'd never thought about the tacos, burritos or quesadillas my mom packed for my lunch, except for that they were delicious and spicy and I generally appreciated her efforts. At my old school with my old friends, my lunches were usually a source of envy. Here, apparently, they were the source of ridicule—the butt of some kind of racist joke.

Another guy at their table actually stood up and pointed at me and yelled, "Paco's got tacos! Run for the Border!" As the laughter of the cool kids began to die down, he added this one to rouse them: "Taco Tuesday—Arriba, arriba!"

They all laughed out loud again.

I guess he and his friends didn't realize that it was a Thursday.

Or that the word "Arriba" didn't really work there.

Those bastards seemed to be too caught up in making fun of my name and my Mexican-ness to worry about accuracy or Spanish grammar, or other people's feelings.

I gave no outward response—my only defense was to appear unaffected by their laughter.

This kind of thing didn't happen every day that semester, but it had happened before. I'd drawn strange stares from day one at Walden, and some of my classmates had taken to calling me 'Taco' because it rhymed with 'Paco.'

Other random lowlights of that semester:

One time I was asked, "Hey, Taco, can we borrow some hot sauce?"

And it wasn't even lunchtime.

On the first day, a teacher asked me, "Paco—is that your real name?" He pronounced it 'Pay-co' for the rest of the semester, despite my correction—maybe because it always got a laugh from a few students in the back row.

Around Halloween, I was called "Dia de Los Muertos" as if it were my name.

Yes, the comments were extremely stupid, but they still hurt.

However, as *The Art of War* prescribed, since I was always outnumbered, I chose not to fight. I tried my best to ignore them.

Anyway, that same lunch recess, two minutes after the cool kids had laughed at me—as if the Paco-Taco thing weren't enough—poop fell from the sky and landed directly on my face.

Literally.

No joke.

It happened like this: As I took the first bite of my second taco, a very warm substance splattered just above my right eye. It felt like a large spoonful of runny refried beans had just scored a direct hit on my face. It didn't immediately register as bird poop. What the hell had just happened? I dropped my tainted taco and wiped the muddy, acrid crap from my eye and the right side of my mouth. Yes, my mouth!

There was a slow-motion second of silence.

Time stood still.

I heard a lone scream—no, more of a banshee battle cry—and then an outburst of hooting and hollering. The explosion of student cackling was all aimed in my direction. Amidst all the noise I heard different versions of "Man, look at all that shit on his face!"

The humiliation was overwhelming.

So I did what I imagine anyone in my shoes would do: I covered my face and ran to the nearest bathroom. Of course—in panic mode—I had tunnel vision. I looked only for an escape route, which is why I didn't even notice which bathroom I had entered.

While I hunkered over the sink splashing water on my face, a girl's voice let out a shriek.

"What the hell are you doing in here?" she said, clearly annoyed.

"Oops," I said, scooping handfuls of water on my face, keeping my head down. "I'm sorry. I'm having a really bad day."

"What happened to you?" she asked with a hint of sympathy.

"I just got pooped on," I said.

"Literally?"

"Yeah," I said.

Literal, yes—but it could also have been a metaphor for my whole first semester at Walden.

I looked up from the sink and turned to the girl I was talking to, but my eyes were all waterlogged and everything was blurry.

I could see she was checking herself out in the mirror, applying some lip-gloss as if she were ignoring me. Her hair was pulled back in a ponytail and she was wearing a tank top. As her profile came into focus, I felt even more uncomfortable.

"I'm sorry I'm in here," I told her. "I needed somewhere to hide."

"No problem. I understand," she said and turned from the mirror to face me. "Well, on the bright side, I think getting pooped on symbolizes good luck in Greece."

"Greece?"

I couldn't manage to get another word out.

I must have been mesmerized by her eyes and her lips—actually, her entire face. It was as if her golden brown skin let off a radiant glow. She was absolutely beautiful.

Her name was Naomi Fox.

LOVE

I didn't fall in love with Naomi right at that moment.

I had a few weeks of winter break to think about her and the impossibility of us being together.

To be exact—leaving all logic and realism behind—I fell in love with her on the first minute of the first day of our second semester creative writing class.

Yes, love. I fell in love with Naomi Fox.

Some might say that because I was in 8th grade, I wasn't really in love; that I don't know what I'm talking about; that it was just a crush. "Childish puppy love," they might call it. But nothing could be further from the truth. I loved Naomi more than anyone or anything.

The problem was that Naomi didn't really love me back.

Well, that wasn't the only problem.

TRENT vs. ME

At the time I fell in love with her, Naomi was already in love with Trent Oden (the leader of the "cool kid" table).

Everyone knew it—even the teachers knew it. Naomi and Trent Oden had been boyfriend and girlfriend since the beginning of the year and rumors had been circulating since September that they were already having sex. Yeah, full-on sex! It was almost unbelievable to me—two of my 8th grade classmates doing it!

On the first day in Mr. Holliday's class, our seats were assigned to us. Each individual desk was marked with a post-it note with our first name on it. They—Naomi and Trent—sat on opposite sides of me in the middle of the classroom's singular rows.

Naomi was on my left, closer to the window.

Trent sat just behind my right shoulder, closer to the door.

This situation wouldn't have been so bad if it weren't for that uncontrollable, unpredictable, wonderful, heart-breaking thing called love that struck me with blunt force the moment I sat next to Naomi on day one of that class— That and the fact that Trent was kind of an ass.

Of course, it's going to be hard to tell this story in an objective way if I continually refer to Trent as an "ass." I will give him more credit than that because, to be honest, he deserves it. After all, he was sort of my friend. That's why I included the words "kind of" right before the word "ass." I should also give him more respect than that because I am aware of my own problem in this particular story: Jealousy.

Trent was a popular jock. He was great at sports and very well known because of it. He was also popular because he was a fairly nice guy. Kind of dumb, but nice. Sure, he hung out with jerks, but he wasn't one himself. He smiled a lot and didn't directly annoy, bully, or harass anyone as far as I knew. He also fit the classic knight-in-shining-armor, movie star, super hero description: tall, dark, and handsome. It was obvious that all the girls thought he was very good looking—not just awarded the label "cute," but "hot." All the girls said he was hot, including Naomi.

How could I compete with that?

I was not hot, nor a jock, nor popular, nor anything like a knight-in-shining-armor.

I used to think I was smart—and not a complete loser. That is, before I transferred schools.

I had friends and got pretty good grades at Dolores, but Walden was a different story. Nobody reached out to me and I didn't reach out either—maybe because I was too busy trying to keep up. The classes were harder, the teachers had higher expectations, and the homework load was nearly impossible. For the first time in my life, I was making a real effort and still almost failing. That first semester at Walden I got all-time lows on my report card (Math= D, English= C, and Science= F).

It definitely disqualified me from honor-roll-nerd-status, but I probably looked the part because I paid attention in class and took notes—unlike my classmates.

Most of my fellow students seemed to constantly have their heads in the virtual clouds—FriendMe and whatever else was the online media trend of the month. They had to keep up with their social networks and constant text messaging, even if they were communicating to someone sitting two rows away from them in class.

Yes, in class.

During every lesson they held their expensive cell phones under their desks, sweatshirts, and even behind pages in their textbooks. And they were pretty damn good at not getting caught. It's safe to say that ninety percent of them could care less about what the teacher was saying or what the lesson was about, choosing to check and peck at their phones most of class time.

But I couldn't afford to do that. Literally.

My parents wouldn't buy me a smart phone, or any kind of cell phone, until I was in high school. We weren't rich like everyone else at Walden. So I had no choice but to avoid technological distractions and, consequentially, paid the social price: isolation and ridicule, along with being the new, half-Mexican outcast.

Thus, it appeared to be no contest between Trent and I.

In every scenario, he won. Hands down.

His obvious bond with Naomi was an everyday reminder of that.

MR. HOLLIDAY's CLASS

On that first day of the new semester in Mr. Holliday's creative writing class there was a prompt on the white board. He pointed to it and then read it aloud to us: "Pretend you are writing to an anonymous stranger. Tell them something about you."

He scanned the classroom full of new faces, looked at me, then glanced at the sticky note on my assigned desk with my name on it.

"Paco?" he asked.

"His name is TJ!" blurted a kid in the back—one of those kids that seemed to have acute volume control issues. "He's Taco Jones!"

A handful of students laughed under their breath.

"Do not speak unless called on young man," Mr. Holliday said to the heckler, then he asked me, "Is that true?"

"Not really," I said.

"I'll call you Paco then," he said, shooting a disapproving glare at the heckler. "Paco, would you like to share your response to today's writing prompt?"

No, I thought. I sat there and stared blankly at Mr. Holliday. What's worse—being called "Taco Jones" or being asked to speak in front of the class on day one? *Why was he calling on me? Who wants to share on the first day? What did he want me to say? —That I couldn't keep my eyes off Naomi? I wasn't about to—*

"—Of course you don't," the teacher said, breaking the awkward silence that teachers seemed to enjoy creating. "It's a personal question and it's the first day of class."

Mr. Holliday paused and grinned, scanning the room of mostly inattentive students.

"That's why our first task is to answer this question as honestly and freely as you can, in your notebooks," he said. He paused while students flipped to a fresh page. "And remember, be honest. It's the key to good writing."

I stared at the board: *Tell them something about you.*

If I were being totally honest I would have written something like this:

From the moment I sat down in this class today, before the teacher had said a word or all the students had arrived, I knew one thing without a shadow of a doubt: I love this girl, Naomi Fox. It's hard to describe, but I can feel it in my bones. It's weird. She has special powers.

But I didn't write that because it was embarrassing and way too personal and Naomi was sitting right next to me. So, because I couldn't think of anything else, I followed Holliday's advice to tell the truth. Here's what I wrote:

Dear Stranger:

Some quick facts bout me: I'm skinny, average height, have straight boring dark brown hair, a big nose, an unflattering birthmark on my neck, pigeon-toed feet and hairy arms. (Yes, very hairy arms—easily the hairiest at Walden. Sometimes I even find fruit flies that get stuck in my arm hairs!) So maybe it goes without saying: I have never had a Valentine, or a girlfriend, or a single hint that any attractive female prospects lay ahead of me.

And, for the first time in my life, I feel stupid and poor here at this school. But to say I'm poor would be an insult to my parents and those out there who are truly poor. This might put it in perspective: Sometimes my family has cereal for dinner because there's nothing else. I don't get new clothes, I get my older brother's hand-me-downs. And I rarely have pocket money or lunch money—I have to pack my lunch or starve... I bet no other kids at this school have to worry about these kinds of things... When my parents decided to send me here, it was a big financial burden for them. But they were willing to sacrifice, they told me, and took out a bunch of loans in order to give me a better future. So I can't screw up, but so far, I have been...

Also, if I'm not already pathetic enough for you, Stranger, there's this: Some of my 8th grade classmates call me "Taco" because it rhymes with Paco and tacos are a popular Mexican food. I guess the stupidity and racism of a group of teenage bastards shouldn't be all that surprising. Does it bother me? Yes, of course, but I have to ignore it for now. Maybe someday I will stand up for myself and humiliate them. Or maybe they'll just stop and I won't have to worry about—

"Time's up," Mr. Holliday told us.

NAOMI

On that same first day of class, while she was sitting at her desk, distracted by her phone, I stole a view of Naomi that's been forever imprinted in my memory. I'd peeked in her direction and noticed that the bottom of her white tank top had hiked up over her waistline, exposing the small of her back. Then, almost as if she knew exactly what she was doing, she leaned forward in a way that tugged the waist of her jeans down. That's when—praise the Lord— the top band of her thong poked out just above the waist of her jeans, luring my eyes down to the top of her butt crack for a few glorious seconds before she instinctively pulled her sagging pants up and her tank top back down.

Crazy how that brief visual sent a stream of euphoria through my skinny body. It was incredible! I mean, give me a break. I was a fourteen year-old boy!

As soon as my butt-crack view was over, I immediately closed my eyes as if I were trying to freeze-frame the image in my mind and also decrease the likelihood that someone might catch me staring.

Was I that shallow? Falling in love with Naomi after sitting next to her for one class period and catching a glimpse of her butt crack?

No, of course not.

Somehow I already knew that Naomi was a special girl. I was really curious to talk to her, and her smile told me she had a great sense of humor. I could tell she was smart, too. But I didn't speak to her that first day, so all I can describe is what I saw.

From the feet up: She was wearing grey, vintage Converse all-star shoes—a classic look that could have put her back in the 1960s. They contrasted with the other girls' trendy choice of Tom's, and revealed that Naomi had ageless taste and her own sense of fashion. She wasn't a follower. She was unique. It appeared that she wore no socks, which told me she was a bit of a free spirit. Her jeans (it was a "free dress" day) were dark blue, naturally weathered and tight—but not the kind of tight that looked painful. Her little white tank top was plain and simple, indicating that she wasn't into brand names, nor was she trying too hard. She didn't have to. Her shoulders and arms were a gorgeous bronze tone and completely hairless (the opposite of my arms). Her dark hair fell to her shoulders in two artful, thick braids. Naomi's hair was always different, but that day her style looked labor intensive and really cool—like some character in a Star Wars movie. Her face was immaculate: High cheek bones, full lips, a button nose, and deep, thoughtful brown eyes—the type that could instantly make you lose your train of thought.

I suppose others would describe Naomi first as African-American, or "black."

I would describe her simply as beautiful.

THE NOTE

The scandalous note incident happened on the second day we had Mr. Holliday's class.

Though it was only the first week, the text messaging during class had already gotten out of control.

Maybe I noticed it because I was left out. Missing out. Out of the loop. Maybe they were all commenting on someone's post about me not having a cell phone. Who knows?

Mr. Holliday hadn't explicitly made a rule against electronic devices yet, so students must have taken it as an open invite. They hid their phones underneath their desks and hid themselves behind the adolescent defense that if it wasn't specifically outlawed ("You said no cell phones in class, not *smart* phones"), then it wasn't a hard and fast rule. Pretty dumb logic, but most often it worked on these teachers.

About half way through the period Mr. Holliday finally noticed the amount of online distraction blatantly going on in the middle of his class. It clearly angered him. He stood up from behind his computer and walked to the front of the room.

"I thought I made it clear when this class started," he said to all of us. "Your assignment is to continue writing on the same prompt from last time, and to revise it when you're finished."

Mr. Holliday paused to take a long, dramatic breath. His faced turned from white to pink to red. He wanted to make sure everyone was listening to him.

"—No part of your writing or revising requires you to use a cell phone, smart phone, or any other electronic device," he scolded us. "If you have them out, I will confiscate them."

I didn't have to worry about his warning, but it made me wonder why teachers liked using certain words like "confiscate" so much. They also seemed to really like saying "inappropriate" and "distraction."

As Mr. Holliday scanned the room for any signs of disobedience, I looked at Naomi and noticed that she still had her phone in her hands. She was texting someone, in the zone, seemingly unaware of the world around her. I glanced back at the teacher and saw that his eyes were now locked on Naomi's desk. I guess he wanted to make an example out of her.

"I'll take that," he said, as he approached her desk.

"Um, what?" Naomi said. She hadn't been paying attention to his warning, but Mr. Holliday's big man-hand was already rested on her desk, waiting for her to cough it up.

"This is clearly a *distraction*. I'll put it on the desk by the door and you can grab it on your way out," he said, as if it were a line he'd repeated a hundred times before. "But next time, I'll keep it until your parents come to pick it up."

Naomi looked annoyed as she handed her phone to the teacher. It seemed as though she wanted to yell at him in protest, but she wasn't the loud, defiant, rude type. She simply turned, made eye contact with Trent, and shrugged her shoulders. Even mad she looked gorgeous.

While Mr. Holliday droned on about our writing assignment, I focused on Naomi. She'd gone to writing furiously in her notebook. I wondered WHAT she was writing with such intensity and WHO she was writing to. Then I turned my attention back to the teacher.

"Truth, love and loss," Mr. Holliday told us. "You should write about real experiences, so you can find your voice…"

It made sense, but it was a bit much for a group of 8th graders. He also said that we could and should write down whatever was on our minds; whatever seemed most important to us; whatever we were passionate about (there was another trendy teacher-word: "passionate").

Mr. Holliday explained a lot more about writing, but I doubt that anyone was listening. Even if their eyes were pointed in his direction, they were most likely focused on his sweaty armpits, awkward hand motions, or that his fly was half-way down.

"Hey," Naomi whispered. *Was she really talking to me?*

I was shocked. Her eyes and subtle head nod directed my attention to the folded paper note in her hand. Once she knew I'd seen it—and had peeked at the teacher to make sure he wasn't looking—she reached out her arm and handed it to me.

My hopeful eyes must have asked, 'A note, for me?'

'No,' her expression said. She looked just beyond my right shoulder.

The note was for Trent.

Sure enough, I pulled it in and looked down at the meticulously folded note addressed to Trent. She had drawn a few hearts around his name, which killed me. I gazed back at her for a moment, pretending like the note was for me. Naomi had no idea that she'd already become my fantasy-dream-girl. If she knew, she'd probably be repulsed.

To her, I was the lowly "Taco Jones."

She was with the mighty Trent. They were a perfect couple. *And they were having sex for Chrissake!*

I was ready to pass the note to Trent, but I wanted to make eye contact with him first. Mr. Holliday had ended his lecture and was now leaning over the special ed student right behind Trent, helping him get started with his writing. A handoff at that moment seemed too risky so I glanced back at Naomi. She shook her head and waved me off, sensing that Mr. Holliday would catch us. That's when the end-of-school bell rang out—more like a starter gun than a bell.

It appeared that Mr. Holliday wasn't aware that our class was about to end. Neither was I, but there I was with the note in my hand.

As students made noise zipping up their bags and shifting in their seats, Mr. Holliday quickly reminded us of our homework—"Keep writing!" Then he dismissed the class, except for me.

"Paco, can I speak with you for a minute?" he said. It was more of a command than a question.

"Sure," I said.

Was I really just asked to stay after class? At first I had no idea why. *Damn, had he seen the note? Was I busted for being the courier?* I remained seated and watched Naomi walk out of the classroom. She shot me a worried look as she passed through the door. Trent met her right outside the room. I saw them embrace and caught a glimpse of Naomi talking to Trent—probably about the note—with a concerned look. She glanced back at me again right before Mr. Holliday closed the door.

God, her eyes were powerful. They told me to push the note deep into my pocket, so I did.

Mr. Holliday pulled a chair close to my desk and asked me a few random, chit-chatty questions which, I gathered, were only lead-ups to his big question:

"Paco, do other kids really call you 'Taco'?"—referring to the dumb comment from the previous class.

"Yeah," I said.

"Doesn't it bother you?"

"Kind of..."

I told him half the truth because what could he do about it? Nothing. But at least he was a teacher who cared and was trying to help out a little. Thankfully, it became obvious that he had no clue about Naomi's note—my real concern—crammed into the pocket of my jeans.

"Sorry that your peers can be so cruel," he said.

"What are 'peers'?" I asked.

"Your fellow classmates."

"Oh, it's no big deal," I said. "It's their problem anyways, right?"

"Yes, I suppose it is," he said. "Well, at least you have a good perspective on it, Paco."

"Thanks."

The truth was that there was much more pain behind the racial teasing. I had pushed it into a place where I could ignore it, but not much longer.

"Maybe you should write about it," he suggested.

"About what?" I asked.

"Write about what it's like to be a teenager, in 8th grade, in this school—to be Paco Jones," he said, as if my name were famous. "You have a... a unique perspective, you know."

He didn't describe my perspective as "pathetic" or "underdog" or "Poor-Mexican-alien-in-a-galaxy-of-rich-whiteness." He seemed to have carefully chosen the word "unique" instead.

Up to that point, I'd considered my life pretty boring. In fact, I hadn't really considered my life at all. *Who cares about what happens to me? Had I experienced anything special? Weren't there others who suffered much more than me? And why was this teacher keeping me after class for so long?* I didn't want to listen to his lame teacher euphemisms and adult talk anymore. I tuned Mr. Holliday out. I just wanted to leave.

Mostly, I wondered if Naomi and Trent were still waiting for me (and the note) outside.

But Mr. Holliday was unwillingly in on some strange act of fate, because when he kept me after class for fifteen minutes (rambling about topics ranging from teen bullying to dead European authors, as if he and I had nowhere else to go) it triggered a chain of events that made the next two months of my life unforgettable.

After being stuck listening to Mr. Holliday, I walked outside of his classroom and through the hallways. I had the note in my hand, expecting to see an impatient Naomi or Trent waiting at every turn, but nobody was around. The front entrance of the school was nearly empty and the famous couple was nowhere to be found.

CONFESSION

I read the note.

I couldn't help it. I walked all the way home (almost 3 miles) and tried to forget about the note, but I couldn't. Nothing was on TV. I had nothing to check online and had lost interest in the lone video game I'd owned and overplayed ever since Christmas. With my curiosity burning, I went in my room, closed the door, pulled out the note, unwrapped her intricate geometric fold job, and read:

Hey Trent, I can't believe that jerk just took my phone! I mean, I guess he was just doing his job, but what a time to cut off our messaging session! Anyway, I just wanted to say that I GET IT. I'm not mad at you anymore. I trust that you didn't spread the rumor about us having sex because I know you wouldn't do that kind of thing. It must have been some little kid in 6th grade that saw us making out and just assumed we must be having sex. Or maybe it was Marisa—she hates me. I really don't know. The point is that, though I know you want to do it, and I'm curious about sex too, I also want to wait. Really, I want to wait till I'm 16. The truth is that I don't want to be called a slut and I don't want to FEEL like a slut. I mean, even if some of the girls want to call me a slut behind my back because of the rumors, then let them. They're gossipers with no life and they hate me anyways because they're jealous. I

*know the truth. So do you. It may sound stupid, but I just
need to wait. Then I can say that I lost my virginity in high
school instead of middle school! It may sound weird, but it
matters to me. This is about respect, so you'll just have to
be patient. ;-) Love, Naomi*

I read it one more time through. The worst part of it was
seeing that Naomi wrote "love" and that she might want to
have sex with Trent in the future. *Damn*, those words were
hard to look at. They hurt my soul. But the best part was
that she was denying Trent, being strong, making him
wait, and she was above the vicious rumor mill that the
other girls had been spinning. I liked that she wrote well
and used words like "assume" and "virginity." It showed
that she was smarter—more articulate than most 8th
graders. And, most importantly, now I knew the secret
truth—they weren't having sex! This was big news.

After reading the note a third and final time, and feeling
some of the words stab again with less sharpness, I tried
to fold the note back into its original shape. It wasn't easy.
I must have tried for ten minutes straight but I wasn't able
to get it back to the way it was. The paper was getting
creased and worn and dirty. Then I accidentally ripped the
corner of it. She'd know I'd read it for sure. I was screwed.

Later that night—after I ate dinner with my parents and
successfully dodged all their questions and avoided
mentioning anything that was really on my mind—I got
online and checked FriendMe. It had become part of my

nightly ritual and I didn't even know why. I'd hope for new messages from friends, but rarely had any. I'd scroll through lame comments that my 36 FriendMe "friends" had posted. I would scan their pictures to see what they wanted me to see of their lives; the images they wanted to project to the world. It was usually more like a window into what people thought was cool rather than what actually was cool. Sometimes I would post something that was on my mind, but mostly I'd just message my few real friends from my old school and we'd make fun of what other people had written—their misspellings, embarrassing admissions, trends, endless selfies and other photographic diarrhea.

But that night when I opened my FriendMe page I had something new: a new friend request.

It was from Naomi Fox!

Just the sight of Naomi's image and name on the screen breathed fresh life into me. I clicked, immediately accepted her request, and proceeded to check out her page. Her profile picture was angelic. It was a well-done, extended-arm-selfie of her smiling, alone, outside on a mountain trail. The photo made her look like a natural born model that hadn't yet been discovered (or found a professional photographer). Naomi had a lot of shots like that—solitary yet happy. It made me think that she liked being alone in natural settings, at peace with herself and her thoughts. I liked that image of her. I spent the next thirty minutes examining the rest of her photos— 224 of them to be exact. Some of them were typical teenage shots with her friends, at the mall, at the beach, at family parties. Every picture of Naomi, even the ones where she made goofy faces, was attractive. There were only a few pictures of her and Trent, and those I skipped over quickly, preferring to imagine myself next to her in her solo shots. And, thankfully, there were no ridiculous pictures of her posing in front of her bathroom mirror, or pursing her lips and squinting her eyes, trying to make sexy facial expressions.

She didn't have to try to be attractive. She just was. This made me love Naomi even more.

When I went back to her main profile page I noticed her status: *In a relationship with Trent Oden*. It was enough to deflate my Naomi-stalking high. A few seconds later, a message box popped up. It was from Naomi and her words truly scared me.

Naomi: Hi Paco. Do you still have that note?

Damn. Of course. The note. She didn't really want to be my FriendMe friend. She wanted the note back and its confidential information concealed. She was probably pissed that I still had it, even though it wasn't really my fault. I mean, it was my fault that I decided to read it three times, couldn't re-fold it, tore the corner, and that I was in love with her.

Paco: Yes.

There was an ominous pause while she typed.

Naomi: OK. Good. I was afraid the teacher saw us and took it from you...You didn't read it, did you?

This was the question I didn't want to answer. If yes, then who knew what the consequences would be. If I typed "no," then I'd be starting our relationship off with a lie. Being dishonest was never a good start, so I confessed.

Paco: Yes, I did. I'm sorry.

There was a long pause. No response. *Damn.* Was she so upset that she'd just leave me hanging without a response? Was she already on the phone with Trent, giving him instructions to kick my ass, or was she strategizing a different way to ruin my life? I tried to clarify:

Paco: The note unfolded a bit on its own while it was in my backpack. I read the part that was exposed… then I read the rest. I was too curious. I really apologize.

Yes, I lied a little, but it was necessary. I didn't want to ruin my chances of maybe being friends with her, maybe more. Someday. That one-in-a-million chance...

I waited a full minute for her response. That minute seemed like an hour. It was enough time to visualize my entire life perfectly unfolding with Naomi, the cinematic montage of highlights flashing before me, then crumbling in all of sixty seconds. Her response finally popped up:

Naomi: Hmmm. You've been a bad boy, Paco… but I think I can forgive you. I feel like… well, just call me and we can talk about it. It'll be easier than typing it all… Here's my number: 619-344-XXXX.

THE PHONE CALL

Part of me was ecstatic that Naomi Fox wanted to talk to me. The other part was terrified.

Her phone number? "Call me?" This was too much. What did she want to talk about? What was happening? I rushed into the kitchen to grab the old school phone and bring it to my room. From the living room, my mom glanced curiously at the phone in my hand. She was in her semi-permanent spot on the corner of the couch.

"Who are you calling, mijo?" she said, in her thick Mexican accent, as if she couldn't help asking.

"No one," I said over my shoulder, walking down the hall to my bedroom.

I sat in my room staring at the phone in my hand, then at Naomi's number, then at the note. I put the Beatles *White Album* on shuffle at low volume.

I was stalling. I was afraid of talking to Naomi and saying the wrong thing—making the situation worse than it already was. But after about ten minutes of deliberation, I figured I had nothing to lose because I didn't really know her, I barely knew Trent, and what was the worst that could happen? Trent might beat me up or intimidate me in the halls. She might call me a few bad names. I could deal with that.

No, I couldn't. I was falling in love with her. If I said the wrong thing it could be over…What could be over?! You have nothing going on with her to begin with, dumbass… Okay, I have nothing to lose.

My mind was going in circles. Finally, I counted down from ten—9, 8, 7, 6, 5, 4, 3, 2, 1—and dialed her number.

"Hi, is Naomi there?"

"Yeah, hi! Is this Paco?" Her voice sounded bright and happy. It caught me off guard. I was expecting a soberness or hint of concern in her tone, maybe even anger.

"Yeah," I said, trying to be calm and composed.

"So what happened?" she said.

I told her why Mr. Holliday had kept me after class—about the "Taco" comments, his rambling about writing and dead writers—and that it all had nothing to do with the note.

"Okaaaaay… So you read my note?" she asked.

"Yeah, I'm sorry about that."

"Have you showed it or read it to anyone else?"

"No, of course not. I just feel bad for—

"Okay. That's good," she said. "I mean, it's not good. I really wish you hadn't read it, but…" She paused. "Let me think."

I worried about what was going through Naomi's mind. She seemed okay with it all, not upset or agitated, but it might have been part of a sinister master plan. Maybe she was plotting a way to humiliate me and just had to play it all out in her head before—

"Don't you hate being called names like 'Taco' and 'TJ' and 'Drug Dealer'?" she asked.

"It sucks, but it could be worse, I guess."

"Yeah. At least they don't call you a *black slut*," Naomi said. "That's what some of the 8th grade girls have called me."

"What? They really call you that?" I asked.

It was outrageous. I had heard "slut" before, but never with the racist twist.

"I hear it almost every day in one way or another," she said. "Sometimes it's unspoken, but understood."

"Then why don't you..." I didn't want to complete the question even though she knew I'd read the note and knew about—

"Why don't I tell people the truth?" she said, finishing my thought. "That I'm not a slut—that I haven't had sex with Trent?

"Yeah, why not kill the rumors?" I asked.

"It's complicated," she said. "And those kids at our school are louts anyways."

Louts? I'd never heard that word before either, but I loved the way she put it. I knew exactly who those louts were, too. It was most of our classmates: the rumor mill; the gossipers; the two-faced cheaters who'd do anything to get ahead or get popular. They spread exaggerated and fabricated tales around the school with such excitement that you'd think someone was paying them for it. And, with non-white students, it seemed like their gossip had a strange layer of racism. But Naomi spoke as if she couldn't really be hurt by dumb, adolescent gossip. She was sophisticated and forward thinking, aware that junior high life was temporary—almost over for us. Yet there was still a vulnerable quality in her voice. She was not just my fantasy-super-model-beauty-queen-love-goddess. She was human, she had feelings, and it seemed as though she was being real with me.

"Can I trust you, Paco?"

"Yeah," I said.

"I mean, you need to promise that this stuff stays between us and us only," she said.

"Yes. I promise."

I was surprised and happy that she was opening up to me of all people. Not only was she not mad at me for reading the note, but it was turning into a real conversation.

"Okay, well…" Naomi paused and took a breath. The sound of air exhaling through her nose was more pronounced and heavy over the phone. "You know some of this because you read my note, but here's the reason: I'm not gonna' tell people the truth because everyone already thinks Trent and I are having sex—and all these other false sexual details—and it's changed *his* whole life. I mean kids at school have been treating Trent like he's a god since the news about us has been out. He's a stud, a legend. Even the teachers treat him differently now. It's crazy."

Everything she said was true. Trent had become so famous at our school it seemed as if his fame was going national. His FriendMe page had thousands of followers. Students, parents and teachers treated him with a certain reverence.

"Anyway," Naomi went on, "And this is the secret weird part—I don't want to ruin that for him. If I did, he'd be crushed and I don't want to lose him because of a few dumb haters who want something to gossip about."

"So you're sacrificing your own reputation and image for Trent?" I asked.

"Yeah. I guess so," Naomi said.

"I don't get it," I admitted.

"Let me put it this way," she said, "Trent's ego has been inflated. His social status has risen more than ever before and he's super popular now. But he's just a boy. To be honest, I can see his weaknesses. If I end the rumor it will deflate his self-esteem, and he'll be devastated. He won't know how to cope, Paco. He'll probably hate me and dump me, then spread even worse rumors about me behind my back. Don't worry about me though, Paco. My self-respect is fine. I'm fully aware of what I'm doing."

"Wow," I said. "You sound like a psychologist or something. Impressive."

"Not really, but thanks," she said. "By the way, I think you're pretty smart too, Paco."

Ahhh, her words were so sweet, her voice so angelic. Was she the least bit aware that her simple compliment had sent a tingly sensation up my spine and butterflies to the base of my neck? Or was she just trying to pump up my esteem and get me on her side? After all, now I knew her precious secrets.

"It's pretty selfless of you to take all of this on for Trent's sake," I said.

"Well, it's kinda' strange to be saying this stuff out loud—admitting that I'm riding the cool kid train—but it's true." She paused. "I guess I like Trent enough to make some small sacrifices," she said.

'Like?' I thought you loved him?" I asked.

Though I probably shouldn't have dared ask a question so bold, it was a logical step. But Naomi hesitated long enough to make me feel uncomfortable and wish I hadn't said what I'd just said.

"I do love him," she said. "I think."

I think? Was this long phone conversation really happening, and what did it mean? There was a moment of silence between us, then a loud voice from outside my bedroom door.

"Mijo, have you done your homework yet?" my mom yelled. I tried to cover the phone so Naomi couldn't hear her. It was the worst possible timing. "Who are you talking to, Paquito? It better not be long distance, *mijo!*"

Embarrassment ran through by body like a wave. I shoved the phone under a pillow, rushed to the door, and cracked it open before my mom let herself in and ruined the best phone conversation of my life. I frantically poked my head out and told her that I'd be off in a minute, that I was talking to a friend—and it wasn't long distance. I wanted to tell her that the concept of long distance wouldn't really exist anymore if she'd get me a cell phone, but it wasn't the right time. Naomi was waiting for me under my pillow.

"Okay, mijo, calm down," my mom said. "Just wrap it up and get ready for bed soon, *por favor.*"

I darted back to the phone. "Hi, are you still there?"

"Yeah, was that your mom?" Naomi said, with a little laugh.

"Uh-huh. Very embarrassing," I said.

"Isn't at least one parent always embarrassing though?"

"Yeah, I guess," I said.

She put me at ease. Her words were kind and understanding. I was melting as I imagined holding Naomi in my arms. I envisioned our first kiss and a big hug, going to the movies together, then driving along the coast in our convertible. I mean, true, I didn't have a convertible. I couldn't even drive a car yet, but I could dream.

"Well, thanks Paco. It was really nice talking to you," she said with a new hint of distance in her voice. "And please remember to keep all this a secret. Don't tell anyone, no matter what. Will you promise me?"

"I will," I said.

I would have done anything for her. She could have asked me to jump off a bridge, or fight a pack of hungry wolves, or swallow a tarantula for her, and I would've done it in a heartbeat.

Before Naomi hung up, she heard the Beatles background music playing in my room: "*Sit and wait a lone-ly life-time...If you waaant me tooo, I will...*"

"Wait, I love that song!" she said. "I don't have that one downloaded yet, but it's on the *White Album*, right?"

"Yeah. It's called 'I Will'," I said.

"Hmmm. Well isn't that a crazy coincidence," she said. "You just told me 'I Will'!"

"Yeah, weird," I said.

"I love the Beatles," Naomi added, "But not their poppy, cheesy, early stuff."

"Me too!" I absolutely agreed.

"But what's a Mexican boy doing liking a band of Brits from Manchester, England?"

She'd caught me off guard.

"You're joking, right?" I asked.

"Of course, Paco," Naomi said. "Black girls aren't supposed to like the Beatles either."

We both laughed in a way that only people who've been stereotyped can understand.

"Damn," I said. "I guess we're both weirdos."

"For sure. Well, I'm glad we talked," she said. "See you later, Paco."

We'd had a good conversation. She had said my name.

I was lying there, floating above my mattress.

Love felt no gravity.

I listened to that Beatles song, "I Will", on repeat for the rest of the night until I drifted off into a deep, wonderful sleep.

SHAKESPEARE

It took me a few days to come back down to earth after that phone call with Naomi. And down I came, back to harsh reality—for what else comes after the highest of highs but the lowest of lows?

In those next days at school I was reminded of a few simple, depressing facts:

1) My two best friends in the world—Juan and Jason—went to different schools across town, so I didn't have any real friends I could trust at Walden.

2) My teachers seemed to treat me as either an invisible presence in their class or as "Taco Jones," the primary Mexican representative in their midst; the kid who wasn't very smart but could recommend authentic Mexican restaurants, got looked at if Dia de los Muertos was ever mentioned, and make them think twice before they said anything about "illegal aliens."

3) Trent and Naomi appeared to be a painfully happy couple, and she obviously cared more about me keeping her big secret than becoming a friend of mine. That week when I'd pass her in the halls, or make eye contact with her in Mr. Holliday's class, all she'd do was give a quick smile or say hello and promptly look away. She was being polite, but not friendly. A few times she'd say "What's up?" or "How's it goin?" but it always seemed

like a brush off—another way to give me a brief "Hi-and-Bye."

But exactly one week after the phone call with Naomi, I made a glorious breakthrough in Mr. Holliday's writing class. There was no writing prompt that day. He'd simply written the word "BRAINSTORM" on the whiteboard in huge capital letters. He stood by the board with a solemn expression on his face that was supposed to hint that class was about to begin. He awkwardly waited for the chatty students to quiet down.

"Okay. Today we're focusing on brainstorming," he said in an uninspired, monotone way that suggested he didn't want to be teaching that afternoon. "For this assignment, you'll talk with a partner. It can be about your writing ideas or anything, really. Remember to be open-minded and honest and the rest will come to you. Now, I've chosen your partners…"

What the heck was he talking about? What were we supposed to do, just talk to our partner? This was his lesson plan? Would it be graded? What a crock of—

"…Paco and Naomi," he said.

Yes, by the grace of God, Mr. Holliday partnered me with Naomi Fox. Suddenly, I could care less about the assignment. Trent ended up getting paired with some guy who always wore dark hoodies and picked his nose a lot. I didn't know his name and I didn't care. I was paired with Naomi! When Mr. Holliday was done reading the partner list, I moved my desk to face Naomi's. She looked at me with questioning eyebrows.

"This is a pretty stupid assignment, huh?" she said.

"Yeah, seems like it," I agreed. Of course, I would agree. I would've agreed if she'd told me the sun orbited around the earth and that climate change was a myth.

"I guess it's okay, as long as we don't have to write much," she said. "And thanks for being cool on the phone the other night."

"No problem," I said.

Hadn't I acted much closer to the opposite of cool? And Naomi was a bit off. It had been exactly seven days since we talked on the phone.

"Is our little pact still intact?" she said and winked at me.

"That's a fact," I said.

"Oh, aren't you clever," she said. "You can bust rhymes, Paco." She looked at me as if trying to figure out a mystery. "Got any creative story ideas?" she asked with less interest. "That's what we're supposed to talk about, right?"

"Yeah," I said. *You,* I thought. *I want to write about you, Naomi.* "I'm thinking about writing a story that takes place in a school."

"Sounds kinda' boring."

That's when—for the sake of trying to sound like an asset to our partnership—I explained to her that I wanted to write about a character who comes to a new school and has a hard time adjusting to bullying, and then finds out that all the bullies are really zombies and vampires, but as my regurgitated plot pitch left my mouth it felt like total crap. It wasn't what I really wanted to write about.

I noticed Naomi zoning out, looking out the window as a ray of bright sunlight broke through the clouds like the cover of a religious textbook.

"What light through yonder window breaks?" Naomi said softly—almost a whisper.

"It is the east, and Juliet is the sun," I responded without thinking. *What?! Where did that come from?*

She turned to me and smiled a great big smile. "Wow," she said, "You know Shakespeare?" Her eyes sparkled.

"Yeah—"

No, I don't. That *Romeo and Juliet* quote was like a complete fluke. *Why?* Over Christmas break I'd heard those lines in a movie over and over because my friend Jason had to memorize part of it for his literature class. I was staying at his house that weekend so I had to listen to that Romeo and Juliet scene to the point of nausea, but I guess I'd ended up memorizing some lines by default. I had no idea they would ever come in so handy.

"—A little bit," I said, not wanting to admit the less impressive truth.

"That's awesome," Naomi said as she reached into her book bag. "We've been reading Romeo and Juliet in my AP Lit class and I'm actually getting into it—ya' know, after we've translated Shakespeare's English into normal English."

I nodded in what I hoped would look like thoughtful understanding. I wanted to connect with her. She was gorgeous and bright. I wanted her to think I was smart, too.

The next thing I knew, Naomi had pulled out her *Romeo and Juliet* copy, opened it to a specific page and said, "I'm gonna' test you then, Romeo." Naomi smirked at me. *Was she flirting?* Her eyes scanned the page. When she found the right line, she held up the book so the only thing I could see was the cover.

She asked, "What comes after this?" and recited:

> *"Arise, fair sun, and kill the envious moon,*
> *Who is already sick and pale with grief*
> *That thou, her maid, art far more fair than she."*

She held her finger on the page and closed the book. It was a true test—a ridiculous challenge for anyone our age. Luckily, it was also from the one scene that I had unintentionally learned. I responded almost automatically:

> *"The brightness of your cheek*
> *would shame those stars*
> *As daylight doth a lamp; your eye in heaven*
> *Would through the airy region stream so bright*
> *That birds would sing and think it were not night."*

Naomi's eyes were wide open with surprise.

"Say it, again!" she said, opening the book to the same page. I repeated the lines without a hitch. She didn't say a word.

I closed my eyes, afraid that my freakish ability to recite that stanza—and only that part—would not be considered very cool. Why was she not saying anything? Was I too nerdy now? Was it obvious that I was in love with her? Was Shakespeare backfiring on me?

"Uh, did I get it right?" I asked.

"That's very impressive, Paco. And what a way to describe Juliet's beauty," she said and paused. "You said it almost perfectly."

"Yeah, well I'm surprised I even got that much," I said. "So what did I mess up?"

"You said 'you' instead of 'her'," Naomi said with her playful grin.

"What?"

"You said: 'The brightness of *your* cheek would shame those stars.' Are you trying to tell me something, Paco?"

That's when I felt half the blood in my body rush to my face. My skin was fairly brown, but I sensed the sharp heat of embarrassment firing like Hot Tamales in my cheeks, making them as red as they could get. I felt warm and clammy and couldn't speak. I wanted to jump out of my seat and run out into the hall.

Before I could escape, a swift pat on my back startled me. It was Trent.

"Sharing some deep thoughts over here, guys?" Trent said.

His emphasis on "deep" carried a tone of ridicule for anything below the surface.

"Just a little Shakespeare talk, babe," Naomi said.

"Oh, Jesus Christ, you've gotta' be kiddin' me," he said. "I hate that crap."

"Back to your seat, Trent," Mr. Holliday chimed in from across the room.

Naomi stared at the back of Trent's plaid shirt as he walked away—a look of disgust, if you ask me. She didn't seem to like how he'd interrupted and belittled our Shakespearean moment. She turned back to me and smiled.

"I think it's great that you know Shakespeare, Paco," Naomi said.

I loved the way she said my name, Pa-co, with an attempted Spanish accent, like I was foreign and interesting.

"What do you think that line means?" she asked.

"Well, I haven't thought about it too much," I said. "But I guess it means that your—I mean, Juliet's—cheeks, face, spirit and everything about her was more beautiful than Romeo could have dreamed up. Her beauty lit up the night sky, it was more powerful than he could imagine."

I'd slipped again with my use of pronouns, giving away that I was focused much more on Naomi than Juliet, but she seemed to like it. I only mention this because Naomi blushed a bit and appeared to be taking my comments as a direct compliment. That was fine by me as long as I wasn't stepping over the line, or making a complete fool of myself. I glanced over my shoulder to see where Trent was. I saw him looking down, writing intently in his notebook.

"Don't worry about him," Naomi told me.

"Huh?" I turned back to her.

"I said, don't worry about Trent." Naomi's voice was hushed so nobody around us could hear. "He just gets a little insecure when people his age talk about academic topics, like Shakespeare, with any real interest."

"He gets good grades though, doesn't he?" I said.

"Yeah, but he just does enough work to get an A. He doesn't really think or care about the meaning. So I guess it scares him when—wait," Naomi stopped herself. "Why am I telling you this?"

"Well, we do have an agreement," I said, "—a promise. You're telling me because you know and trust that I will keep your secrets."

I was desperate for her to keep talking to me—anything to be around her, even if I had no chance of ever being more than just the nice guy in class who would listen to her.

"I can promise you that I'll never share anything you tell me with anyone. It won't be too hard for me—I don't have any friends here, anyway."

She laughed and added, "I don't have many friends, either—not ones I can trust."

Damn. "Really?" I asked.

"Yeah." She hesitated, peeked over toward Trent's desk, and continued in an even lower voice: "Trent doesn't really have a clue about me. It's so frustrating. All he talks about is himself, basketball, people he likes and dislikes, and how much he likes me—but it's all so superficial. All I want is a little intelligence and sensitivity, a little more depth... But I can't really talk to anyone about all this because I feel like they'll broadcast it and it'll just turn into gossip against me."

"Can I ask you something?" I whispered. "Will you promise not to take it personally?"

"Yeah, go for it," she said.

"Why do you even like Trent?"

Naomi paused as if she were wondering if she was offended or not. I regretted my question for a moment, but what had gotten me on the phone and talking to her in the first place? I had nothing to lose.

"He's popular, he's hot, he's got ambition, he seems like he's going places," she said. "God, that sounded worse than him! Ugh."

It did, but I didn't say anything. We were all caught in our middle school webs of hormonal, social, and self-confusion, so who was I to judge? I turned to look at Trent again, afraid that he might be right behind me.

"He likes you, ya' know," she said.

"What? Trent?" I asked, shocked I'd been a topic of conversation. "Why?"

"He told me you're a nice guy who doesn't really care about much. He's the competitive type, so you pose no threat to him—anyway, that's my amateur psychoanalysis. You're not obsessed with sports, you don't get the best grades—" she cut herself off, maybe aware that her observations about me might be a bit insulting. "That's why I'm surprised—delightfully surprised—that you know and understand Shakespeare."

I tried to explain that I happened to know only that one part of *Romeo and Juliet*. It was all the truth, but Naomi cut me off.

"—Gimme a break. You quoted a whole sonnet," she insisted. "So you're smart, sensitive, and modest. That means you're gonna' make a good girl very lucky some day, Paco."

Could that girl be you, Naomi? Will it be you? Why are you still with Trent for all the wrong reasons? I was dying to ask her these questions but had to control myself.

"Thanks," I said.

That's when Mr. Holliday ended our brainstorming session. "Now, everyone get back to your assigned seats," he said.

I was torn. Part of me felt like stabbing Mr. Holliday with my pencil for ending my chat time with Naomi, but the other part felt like thanking him profusely for partnering us. I stood up and smiled at Naomi.

"*Tenemos un pacto?*" she asked, referring to keeping her secrets confidential.

"*Si, en facto,*" I said, grabbing my notebook and pencil.

"*Bueno.* And way to bust rhymes, Paco."

"Thanks," I said, "But why are you speaking Spanish?"

"Well, I know a little and I figured you knew some too," she said.

"Ah, because I'm Mexican, right?" I asked with a playful grin.

"Oh, snap. That's kinda lame, huh?" she said, pouring on the vernacular. "Like people comin' up on me speakin' all ghetto just cuz I'm black."

"Yeah, but it's no problem coming from you, Naomi," I said, then continued half ashamed. "The sad thing is that I'm not even fluent in Spanish."

"Don't sweat it, Paco," she said sweetly. "I'm not fluent in Black or Ebonics or whatever-it's-called. And, because I'm not poor, some people don't think I'm *really* black."

We both laughed.

A few seconds later, when every student was settled and quiet in their seats, Mr. Holliday spoke to the whole class: "I hope—after discussing with your partner—you've come up with some good ideas for writing topics. I just want to share one very encouraging thing I heard over here from Naomi and Paco..."

What! Damn, he heard what we were saying? Did he have bionic ears? What part of our conversation had he eavesdropped on?

He continued: "I was glad to hear them mention *Romeo and Juliet* because Shakespeare is one of my favorites. I don't love reading his antiquated language, but he did what all truly great writers do," he said. "He told us the truth."

Maybe so, but all I knew for sure after Mr. Holliday's class was that—like Romeo— I was madly in love, and not only with Naomi's exterior. We'd opened up, connected to each other, and shared something meaningful. Had I miraculously moved from the loser guy who inconveniently read her private note, to someone who'd caught her interest and she could trust?

Another positive: She didn't seem phased by my skinny legs, hairy arms, or lack of cell phone.

BASKETBALL

That afternoon we had basketball practice.

I know I've mentioned that I wasn't athletic or into sports—and I wasn't—but that didn't keep my dad from insisting that, for the sake of a "healthy balance," I should play one sport during the school year. Forced to choose, I picked basketball because it was the game I was least horrible at. Unlike the other sports, I knew the basic rules and could dribble the ball a little without losing control. But I couldn't shoot and I had none of the "aggressiveness," "poise" or "footwork" that Coach Huskie always talked about. In fact, I didn't understand half the sports lingo that came out of Coach's mouth.

None of this mattered much because when it came to the games (there'd been three since December), I never played. Coach would pick the starting five (the same five players he always chose) and I would sit on the bench for the rest of the game and daydream about myself on the court, playing like a superstar. I'd never gotten into a real game, only scrimmages at practice, and even then it was for the last two minutes when one team was either winning by twenty points or losing by the same margin. If my all-time game highlights were being filmed they'd look more like a lowlight blooper reel: Traveling violation. Missing an easy shot. Kicking the ball out of bounds. Committing a pointless foul with Coach shaking his head. Game over.

Anyway, that day, while I was lacing up my shoes in the locker room before practice started, Trent sat down next to me and patted me on the back—something he'd never done before.

"Hey, Paco. What's up?"

"Hi," I said. I was scared. What did Trent want with me? Did he know that I'd talked to his girlfriend two times in the past week, had become her FriendMe friend, and knew their number one secret?

"Hey man, can I talk to you after practice?" Trent asked.

"Yeah, no problem,' I said. *Damn.* He might as well have asked if I'd be available to get my ass kicked in an hour or so. *What did he want with me after practice?*

That afternoon's practice was the longest of the entire season. Each minute seemed like an hour—maybe my final hour. How crappy would it be if I spent my last minutes on earth playing a game that I had no real interest in and wasn't any good at?

But, maybe because I was convinced that Trent would kill me after practice, I played some of the best basketball of my life. I didn't make my shots, but I made some good passes and dribbled around defenders like never before. Coach even directed some "Nice job!" comments my way, and I knew they were aimed at me because he said them with a surprised tone—not the way he usually praised Trent or Alan Jacobson, the team's co-captains.

—

"Atta' boy! That's it Trent, take 'em! That's the way it's done boys. Watch Trent!" Coach Huskie would repeat throughout practice. It was as if he wanted to adopt Trent as his son for no other reason than his ability to play basketball.

And he could play. Trent averaged 20 points per game, a little more than Alan, and more than half of what the whole team would score in a single game. He also played good defense, blocking shots and stealing the ball straight from the other players' hands. We'd only played three games, but after each one the coach of the opposing team would single out Trent and shake his hand, treating him like a foreign dignitary. Trent would take pictures with opposing players, coaches, refs and random people in the bleachers. One time I even saw him autograph a basketball for a young fan.

So as practice came to a close, I figured it might not be the worst thing in the world to get my butt kicked by Trent Oden. He might just end up playing in the NBA, and then I could watch him on TV and tell the people around me that he'd kicked my ass back in junior high because I dared talk to his girlfriend.

"Okay, on the baseline!" Coach yelled. "Suicides!"

At the end of every practice we'd line up on the baseline of the court and have to sprint to the free throw line, touch it, sprint back to the baseline, touch it, run to the half court line, touch it, and so on, until we were so tired we could barely breathe. The more we ran the more I wanted to know why these sprints were called "suicides." Torture, yes, but suicide? If I had elected to do these hellish sprints on my own then I might call them suicides, but it wasn't my choice. Coach seemed to want to separate the strong from the weak, and I wasn't exactly passing his test.

"Taco—Paco, whatever the hell," Coach Huskie yelled out, "Do you have lead in your shoes?"

I shook my head. *Damn.* I couldn't believe that bastard had called me "Taco." He was a teacher for Chrissake! Teenage boys were expected to be idiots, but adults should know better.

"On the baseline again!" he screamed, as if we'd all done something horribly wrong. "This will be the last suicide, unless Taco-man over here comes in last again."

Half the kids on the team laughed. I heard a few of them repeat "Taco," but most were too out of breath to say anything.

"Ready," Coach yelled. "Go!"

I kept my face forward and focused on running my absolute hardest. I should have had an advantage. I was skinny and had long legs. The only problem was that I was a bit uncoordinated. My feet were too big for my body. I envied the other boys' quickness and agility. I didn't have that. Most of them moved like cats— I moved more like an ostrich. So all the stop and go action made me appear slower than I actually was. On the final sprint back I was close to the last one in the pack, but I wasn't. I could feel some one right on my tail. We passed the end line and I'd made it in before him. It was Trent. What? How was that possible? Had he injured himself? Or had he done it on purpose?

"Are you goddamn kidding me, Trent?" Coach said at an uncharacteristically low volume. "You let Taco beat you?"

Trent said nothing, as if he were challenging Coach—because what could he do to Trent that wouldn't hurt the whole team's chances of success?

"Well, come out here to the free throw line and make up for it," Coach Huskie said, passing the basketball to Trent. "Fourth quarter, gentlemen. The game is on the line. Trent here needs to make two free throws to win it and make up for his mistake. If not, more suicides."

The whole team sighed in agony. Trent dribbled the ball to the free throw line. He flashed an arrogant smile at us—his teammates' rosy, panting faces. He bounced the ball once, bent his knees, and shot in rhythm. He made the first basket, then the second.

Practice was over and I didn't know whether to be glad or scared to death. Trent walked straight to me and I stood there, frozen.

"Don't worry, dude," he said. "I just need some advice and I think you can help me out."

THE ADVICE

After I managed to change my clothes without any one else in the locker room seeing me naked, I walked out to the front of the gym where Trent was waiting for me. He sat on the steps with his notebook from our class lying next to him. His pose was non-threatening.

"Nice practice today, Paco," he said.

"Thanks," I said, unsure if he was being sarcastic or not. "Did you lose that last suicide on purpose?"

Trent smirked. "Yeah, I couldn't let you lose, man. You know, I try to do what's best for the team." I suppose it could've sounded noble, but the way it came out of Trent's mouth sounded like a quote from some pro athlete who was unaware of his own colossal ego.

"So, Paco, I've noticed that you and Naomi have become friends lately."

"Yeah, kind of," I said, afraid of what was coming next.

"Well, I think it's a good thing," he said. "You're a good guy and she needs someone to talk to about all that smarty-pants stuff like Shakespeare and crap."

Very articulate, Trent. But the good news was, like Naomi had said, he apparently liked me. In other words, he didn't want to kill me. I was "non-threatening." I was a horrible basketball player and an unattractive human being. To him I was nothing more than a Mexican loser who could talk to Naomi about nerdy stuff that didn't interest him.

"Thanks," I said. He didn't pick up on my sarcasm.

"*No problemo,* dude," Trent said.

I'm sure he had no idea how annoying it was when white people spoke to me in half-assed Spanish.

Trent opened up a notebook labeled "Creative Writing," snapped the pages back until he got to the right one, and said: "I'll just let you read this so you can understand my predicament, bro." He handed over his notebook and I read it to myself:

We're supposed to write the truth. Well, ok, here's the truth. I have a really hot girlfriend and I need to get her a good Valentine's day present because she's hinted at it a few times and there's a big dance on that day and I need to be ready. The thing is, I don't know what the hell to get her. I mean, I could get her something sexy like a bra and panties, but this might backfire on me. I don't want her to think I'm a dirty scumbag. I want to impress her. It has to be good and maybe expensive. There's a cool Lebron James basketball DVD I could get her because she told me she likes him, but I don't know.... Mr Holliday, you said you wouldn't judge this so I'm trusting that you won't. If you are reading this and it isn't the type of thing I can write in your class then I will write something different. I just want to get a good grade so please tell me how I can do this if this entry is not to your standards—

"Did you finish yet? —Get the point, Paco?" Trent asked.

"Yeah, I got it."

Naomi was right on. Trent was clueless. Bra and panties? I mean, who even says "panties"? And a basketball DVD of Lebron James? Really? I'd never been close to having a girlfriend yet, but even I knew the Lebron James DVD was a horrible gift idea.

"Can you help me?" he asked.

He sounded much more desperate than I would expect from a junior high icon. And then it hit me: He wasn't the legend that everyone thought he was, and he knew it. He'd never had sex with Naomi, and she didn't really love him. He was only physically bigger than everyone else because he'd hit his growth spurt early. His parents were filthy rich and spoiled him with everything he used to impress others. Probably half the things that made Trent so popular were not based on his achievements, but based on luck and lies. And here he was proving it, asking me to give him the keys to the castle, the last puzzle piece so he could have a chance at de-virginizing Naomi!

"Just tell me what to buy her," he said.

I was right. He was counting on me. It was an empowering realization. He thought he could buy Naomi, and he was dead wrong. I could've told him anything, and I was tempted to tell him to go ahead with the basketball DVD and lingerie, but I knew it wouldn't work. Naomi would hate it and he'd come blaming me. It would be too obvious. If Trent wanted my advice, I'd give it to him.

Taking what I'd learned from a few movies and TV shows, I told him it wasn't about buying Naomi something as much as it was about showing her that he paid attention to her, listened to her, and cared about her interests. Trent looked back at his notebook then shot me a confused stare. I told him that Naomi would be impressed by two things: a thoughtful letter that showed his deeper side— maybe even a reference to Romeo and Juliet or some other classic lines—and music that was dear to her heart.

A good Beatles album? This would win her over and give him a leg up. I knew she would like it, and wished I had the courage to give her the gift myself.

"Really?" Trent said, sounding skeptical.

"Yeah. 100%," I said.

"Can you help me write the letter?" he asked.

"What?"

"You heard me."

"Yeah," I said. "I guess so."

"Awesome, amigo."

He stuck out his hand. We shook on it.

And that was that. I had become Naomi's confidante and Trent's Cyrano in less than three hours, yet neither one of them knew my role as a double agent. I didn't really want the Trent connection, but it was hard to say no to him. He was famous and all-powerful in our junior high world, even if I could now see through his facade. He was still the almighty Trent. I grabbed my backpack and walked away from the front steps of the gym. Trent lounged there waiting for his mom's brand new Range Rover to pick him up.

"Hey, Paco," Trent called. "You've got a decent shot, but you need to shoot to make it."

"What?" I asked, turning back.

"I'm talking about your basketball shot, bro," Trent said. "You're shooting to not miss the rim. You're afraid of missing. Relax. You should practice shooting to make it, instead of shooting to not miss."

I nodded and waved to Trent as I started my long walk home. On the way, I thought about Naomi's encouraging words, Trent's weaknesses, and my shot.

THE LETTER

I really didn't have a clue what to write to Naomi, but I was on the job for Trent and I couldn't disappoint. Naomi liked The Beatles and Romeo and Juliet, so I needed to work from there, keep it on Trent's level, and hope for the best.

Yeah, that was my crappy plan.

The problem was that a Beatles song off the *White Album* might be too obvious. And it would take awhile to find lyrics I wanted on other albums, and who knew if she'd think they were cool or not. Shakespeare, on the other hand, might come off as more thoughtful, romantic and sophisticated. Naomi might be impressed by it. But would she think that I had anything to do with it? She hadn't ever seen me talking to Trent. Romeo and Juliet was world famous for romantic lines. She'd really have no reason to think it was me, unless I told her or someone else was spying on me.

A few days went by and it became obvious that I was over-thinking it. Finally, I got to the point where I understood that anything half-way thoughtful would be a step up for Trent and greatly appreciated by Naomi. I went online and searched for a Romeo and Juliet scene. The first time I scanned through it, the words made no sense to me. But the second time through I focused on this part:

"Romeo: With love's light wings
did I o'er-perch these walls;
For stony limits cannot hold love out,
And what love can do that dares love attempt;
Therefore thy kinsmen are no let to me.
Juliet: If they do see thee, they will murder thee.
Romeo: Alack, there lies more peril in thine eye
Than twenty of their swords: look thou but sweet,
And I am proof against their enmity."

Yeah, I had to look up some words and check a few study guides. But once I got the gist, I thought about Trent's situation. I was the only one who knew he hadn't had sex with Naomi. She had set up a wall. No sex, she'd said, until she was sixteen. But with "love's light wings," he wanted to get over her walls. Her "stony limits" could not hold his love out.

In a weird way, it worked! But I couldn't directly quote Romeo and Juliet. It might have come off as cheesy and scripted. If I interpreted it and applied it to Naomi, she would never believe Trent would go in that direction. So I decided to dumb down the words, rip off Romeo's main ideas and pawn them off as Trent's.

This is what I wrote for him:

Dear Naomi: You may not realize this, but I love you more than you can possibly imagine. You may not see it, but I get nervous when I'm in your presence, chills run up my arm when I hold your hand, my heart smiles inside when I hear your voice. That's what love can do. Amazing things. Love's wings set me floating above you and you don't know that I'm thinking, caring, trying to be a better person, for you. No barriers or locks or classroom clocks can stop this momentum between us (hey, that rhymed!). The next time I see you, beware of your eyes. There's more power in them than you realize. They make me float, and dream... Love, Trent

It was strange writing "Love, Trent" but I knew he might screw up even the smallest details, so I kept it in there. I emailed the note to Trent the next day. Valentine's Day was right around the corner. It was weird taking on the double agent role, and it made me ask: *Am I being a total coward for not stepping up and telling Naomi I love her myself?*

Yeah, I was, but I was convinced that the timing wasn't good.

I had to wait for the right moment.

VALENTINE'S DAY

Up until that point in my life, I had no idea what kind of shit storm I was capable of producing. Like most bad word expressions, I learned "shit storm" from my older brother (so much older, he'd already moved out and gone away to college out-of-state). *Shit storm*. I think it's a fitting description for what happened on that Valentine's Day.

When I walked into the school lobby that morning, I noticed a colorfully handwritten poster advertising the student council's sale of Valentine's Day candy-grams. It made me already regret what I had done the day before. Because I had given Trent the advice to give Naomi a thoughtful card with Romeo and Juliet paraphrased quotes, along with red roses and the Beatles "Revolver" CD, I knew I couldn't give her the same thing. But I'd wanted to give Naomi something. I had to.

Give—that's what true love makes you want to do.

Since I didn't want her or Trent to know, I'd sent Naomi—in an impulsive, semi-courageous moment—13 anonymous candy-grams. Why 13? I bought as many as I could with the $5.50 I'd collected for lunch money over the week. It was the best way to show her my affection (obsession?) without risking too much or causing any problems, right?

Wrong.

The candy-grams were sent out to the students during our first period homeroom class. Naomi wasn't in my homeroom, but I could picture her getting them. The lollipops were red and heart-shaped, and the cards were pink and white with big hearts on them. The day before, I had given the student council kid in charge of the candy-grams the completed order form. I had written 'Anonymous' on the 'FROM' line and the quote 'Who knows how much I love you?' in the personal 'NOTE' section. It was a lyric from the Beatles song "I Will" that I knew Naomi liked. It seemed bold yet safe. She might make the connection or she might not. But if that one "I Will" moment we had on the phone was as special to her as it was to me, then she would remember and would respond accordingly. If she didn't recognize the reference, then no harm done—right?

Wrong again.

It might have worked if that student council bastard hadn't disregarded my personal note request and instead, inside all of my 13 candy-grams, wrote "Be Mine." *Be Mine?* It sounded so possessive and generic. I had no idea that the student card makers would take the liberty of writing in their own messages.

I got one card sent to me from someone named Nicol who I didn't know. It also said "Be Mine." Most people sitting around me got five or more candy-grams. I noticed the other Valentines. The sender's names were written in bold letters but, of the ones I checked out around me, none of them said "Anonymous." Receiving 13 Valentine's cards labeled "Anonymous" with nothing more than "Be Mine" on them might seem a little creepy. It might look like it was sent from some computer hacking weirdo who was up all hours of the night hunched over in front of his screen, stalking people; some Emo freak! Still, maybe it would make Naomi curious, interested to know that there was someone out there who really appreciated her; someone mysterious; someone intriguing.

Wrong again.

I didn't see Naomi until Mr. Holliday's class later that day. I was sitting in my assigned seat, waiting for her to walk in and either wink at me flirtatiously or tell me all about her new, romantic, secret admirer. She walked into class right behind Trent.

"Great, so now I have a stalker," she said.

"That wanna-be-Romeo is a dead man," Trent said.

Naomi grabbed his hand before he sat down. "Don't be stupid, babe," she said. "Fighting someone over something like this? Really? It would be selfish and jealous."

"It would?" Trent said.

Naomi didn't dignify Trent's question with a response. She just shook her head at him, smiled, and went to her seat. I sat there and opened my notebook as if I had some important work to do. I was sandwiched between the tension of Trent's anger and Naomi's disgust. I had no idea if either of them had a clue it was me who had sent the 13 candy-grams. All it would take was one rat in the student council to identify me as Naomi's stalker, and then it would spread like wildfire. Naomi turned in my direction so her legs were almost perpendicular to the front end of my desk.

"How's your Valentine's Day been, Paco?"

"Oh, you know. Pretty uneventful."

"Did you get any candy-grams?" she asked. I didn't like the question for multiple reasons. First, she may have been on to me. *Maybe she already knew I was her stalker?* Other than that, the whole candy-gram thing was like a popularity contest. Who got the most candy-grams today? It was equivalent to posting some picture on FriendMe and seeing how many "likes" you got compared to someone else's posting. It was dumb. It might have been the first thing Naomi had said to me that I didn't enjoy hearing.

"I got... one," I said. It sounded pathetic. It was pathetic.

"Oh. Well, at least you got one," she said. "Do you know the girl?"

"No, I have no clue who she is," I said, "Some girl named Nicol."

"Ohhh. That's too bad for her," Naomi said. "What did it say?"

"Be Mine," I said. "Kinda' lame, huh?"

"Hmm," she said, "Maybe the student council just filled in generic messages if they didn't like the personalized notes?"

"Yeah, maybe," I said.

In her presence, I was starting to melt again. I could care less about the candy-grams. I was just happy to be in close proximity.

"Well, I only say that because I got a bunch of cards today," Naomi went on, "And too many of them said 'Be Mine.' It doesn't make any sense."

"That's weird," I said, trying to go with it.

"Yeah, kinda' creepy coming from someone named 'Anonymous'," she said.

I said nothing. *Kinda' creepy. Damn.*

"Going to the Valentine's dance tonight?" she asked.

"I don't think so."

"You should go. Maybe you'll see Nicol there?"

"Nicol?" I said skeptically. "I don't even know who she is!"

"Maybe she'll reveal herself tonight?" Naomi said. "You never know."

Damn. Her last few words sent butterflies up my neck. *You never know.* Her eyes had the same power as Juliet's from the famous balcony scene—the one I'd ripped off for Trent's sake. I pondered the chance of dating her and, unlike Trent, understanding, respecting, and appreciating her for who she was inside—not just her beauty. From that moment on, as delusional and unrealistic as it may sound, I applied her "You never know" comment to all my hopes and dreams about being her boyfriend someday. Did I have a chance?

You have nothing to lose... You never know.

And for the first time since I'd heard about the Valentine's dance, I actually considered going.

…

I didn't get a chance to talk to Naomi again once class started, but after class Trent found me in the halls. It was the first time he'd intentionally sought me out during school hours, between classes. Naomi was nowhere in sight.

"Thanks, dude. You were right on," Trent said. "I screwed it up though."

"What?" I said. "Did she like the letter I—you gave her?"

"Yeah, she loved it, man. The flowers, too. The Beatles CD made her jump up and down," he said. "But not the hoops DVD."

"—What?" I said, and realized I'd blurted out my question a bit too loud. I lowered my voice. "You gave her the Lebron James DVD?"

"Yeah, and a sexy red bra, too," he admitted. "I thought she'd like the variety, but when she opened them her smile stopped. She called them "random." She looked at me as if I was an idiot. Anyways, it didn't work."

"Didn't work?" I said.

I was young, but already I knew the point of giving gifts should be to find something the receiver would like and appreciate, maybe even, for Valentine's Day, find romantic.

"It's all about the timing," Trent started, "I'm trying to… Never mind, dude."

I got it. Selfishness. He wanted to have sex with Naomi Fox. That was it. His plan was to give her multiple gifts that would sweep her off her feet and shift her attitude so he could steal her virginity and cement his legendary status. It would no longer be just a rumor propping him up. It would be the truth. Trent didn't really love Naomi like I did. He just wanted bragging rights.

I was conflicted. Part of me hated Trent's guts. He had Naomi and he didn't deserve her. He had middle school fame and status, but half of it was based on a lie. Oddly, another part of me felt more popular and special simply to be talking to him in the halls like we were actual friends. I'd never felt that before. Mostly, my existence in the halls of Walden was solitary and soured with the occasional "Taco" comment.

Also, a much smaller part of me sort of felt sorry for Trent. I heard desperation in his voice. His usual confidence wasn't there. Maybe I could notice it now because my own confidence was slowly growing. Was it possible that Trent could be peaking in the 8th grade? That life would all be downhill for him after graduation? Did I have a chance at being more than just average, unpopular "Paco-Taco"? More importantly, did I have a chance with Naomi?

"You going to the dance tonight?" Trent asked.

"Yeah," I said. It came out quickly, thoughtlessly. Something inside my brain must have made the decision without conferring with me.

—

My answer sparked something in Trent. He looked me dead in the eyes, excited, and said: "I have an idea, bro."

TEQUILA

My walk home from school that afternoon consisted of Trent and Naomi's voices echoing the two significant things they'd said to me on that fateful day.

Trent: "Bring some booze. Spike the punch."

Naomi: "You never know."

Bring some booze. Spike the punch....You never know...

It swirled around my brain and repeated too many times.

Finally, it kind of made sense. For whatever reason, Naomi wanted me to go to the dance. She either knew this girl, Nicol, and knew she was going, knew something else I didn't know, or—the most unlikely scenario—Naomi wanted me to be there especially for her for some reason. Maybe she knew Trent wouldn't dance and wanted a nice guy back up? Maybe she wanted someone to talk to when Trent was off hanging with his buddies? Maybe she was planning to break up with Trent and wanted me there to support her! Whatever it was, she wanted me to be at the dance, so I would make it my mission to be there. I'd sneak out of my house if I had to.

Trent's request for alcohol wasn't a shocker. What was shocking about it was that he'd asked me of all people to bring booze to the dance and spike the punch. It was a big responsibility and could carry some heavy consequences, but it would give me a big boost. He said the "Taco" talk would end and the name "Paco" would become the new cool. He made his case to me first in the hall outside Mr. Holliday's classroom and again at the end of school.

"If people get a little buzzed, the dancing will get freaky, girls will start making out with boys, and the dance will turn out to be the party of the century!" Trent said. "And you'll be the one who made it happen, Paco. You'll get all the credit. You'll be the hero of the month and remembered for all time."

I thought about it. Though I could care less about the popularity Trent seemed to cherish so much, I wanted Naomi to pay attention to me, think about me, and ultimately give me a chance. A bit of school-wide celebrity might help me out in that department. Shedding the Taco label would be a nice perk, too.

"Yeah, but if I get caught?" I asked.

"Even better. Then more people will know it was you—and you'd be taking one for the team," Trent explained. "And as far as punishments go, no problem. First offense, they'll give you a slap on the hand, maybe a suspension. Nothing serious."

I knew what Trent's motive was. He wanted to get Naomi drunk and take advantage of her. Period. He didn't care about anything or anyone else. Of course, he didn't say this out loud, but that was the purpose of the alcohol. He figured the booze would loosen her up and he might get past second base with her.

"Why not?" he asked.

It sounded simple and dumb coming from Trent's mouth, but it was the deciding question. If I didn't do anything, then what? Answer: Nothing will happen.

My dad once told me, "Nothing comes from nothing, son," but I had no idea what it meant until the moment Trent asked me: "Why not?"

Ever since I was seated in between Trent and Naomi in Mr. Holliday's writing class, my life had become much more interesting. As hopeless as it once seemed, I was now in love with a wonderful girl. She may not have known it, but that didn't diminish the feelings I had for her. She made me dream. She made me float and gave me hope. She helped me envision the possibility of a much better life. And, though a distant second, the legendary Trent Oden had become an acquaintance, even a friend of sorts. They both had confided in me. They both trusted me for some odd reason. Yes, perhaps they were both using me, but it was better than where I had been before: Bored. Lonely. Ridiculed. Now my stock was rising, and I could either stay on this wave, or pull out altogether.

"Well?" Trent said.

"Why not?" I said. "I'm in."

"Awesome," he said, excited. "I'll email you the details in an hour."

Sure enough, when I got home and checked my email, it was there. The booze plan was addressed to no one and claimed by no one. Even the email address in no way identified Trent as the sender. He'd planned it out with Navy Seal-like precision. I was instructed to find two one-liter bottles of Sprite (or any clear, non-alcoholic, plastic beverage containers). I was to empty them, clean them, and fill the bottles with any strong, clear liquor I could find: preferably gin or vodka. I was to be at the dance at 7pm and go to the table with the punch bowls and snacks at 7:30 sharp, unless I was sent a text message that stated otherwise (They obviously didn't know that I didn't own a cell phone).

My parents weren't home from work yet so it was easy. I found some small plastic bottles, cleaned them, went to the cabinet where they kept alcohol and grabbed the largest bottle I could find. It was Tequila—*1800 Especial Blanco*, 80 proof Tequila to be exact.

The first phase of the operation went down like clockwork. I loaded my backpack with the bottles. They were old water bottles and the Tequila was crystal clear, so it worked out perfectly. I put on one of my newest, darkest pairs of jeans and a clean, unwrinkled collared shirt that had been hanging up in my closet since summer when I'd worn it for a wedding. I finished all my homework early and when my parents came home I showed them the evidence of my hard work, responsibility and maturity, then asked them if I could go to the dance.

"Well, I guess so," my dad said.

"Wait, mijo," my mom interjected. "Is your room clean?"

I couldn't believe my mom. She always insisted that everything be super clean. She never let me leave the house without asking if I had done some domestic chore. I gave her a blank stare. It was 6:35pm.

"As soon as your room is clean, mijo, you can go," she said.

I didn't want to argue. I wasn't the arguing type. I'd watched my older brother argue and fight with my parents and get absolutely nowhere with it. What was the point? The child lost every time, at least in my house. So I ran into my room, threw my clean clothes in one pile and my dirty ones in another. I cleared my desk, the floor, and made my bed. I even vacuumed to create some noise that might even make my mom feel guilty for bribing me into manual labor. I finished at 6:48.

"Bye mom! Bye dad!" I said as I hurried out the front door.

"Bye, mijo! Adios!" my mom yelled. My dad probably said bye too, but I couldn't hear him.

I doubled my walking pace, which turned into a jog all the way to school. My backpack felt heavier and heavier as I went. I had no time to think about my motives or the potential consequences. My only concern was getting there on time (in case you hadn't heard, Mexicans are stereotyped as always being late) and carrying out the mission as planned. I arrived at the Valentine-heart-decorated front doors of the gym at 7:05pm. There were two adults and two kids sitting at a welcoming table. One of the bleach blonde-haired ladies held out her hand to me as I neared the entrance.

"Ticket?" she said.

"Oh," I said, caught off guard. "How much is it?"

"Only five bucks," she said, as if every teenager walked around with a wad of five-dollar bills in their pocket.

"Damn," I muttered.

"Excuse me, young man?"

"Sorry, Miss."

I knew I shouldn't say "damn" in front of adults at school, so I said it to myself a few more times. *Why?* Because I had no money at all. I reached in my pocket. Nothing. I stood there feeling poor and stupid for a few seconds, then wondered if I looked suspicious to them.

"You could go home, get some money, and come back," the other adult woman said, with an air of fake optimism.

I couldn't go back home for multiple reasons. First, there was no way I'd make it to my house and back by the 7:30 sharp start time for Operation Tequila Spike. Second, there was no guarantee that my parents would even give me five dollars. They rarely gave me extra money. I knew how their system worked.

Just as I was beginning to accept defeat, I heard a car pull up behind me and saw all eyes at the ticket table turn. It was Trent being dropped off by his hot mom in their brand new Range Rover. His entourage of three friends piled out of the back seat and strolled up to the front entrance along side him. When Trent saw me he grinned and stuck out his hand for the secret handshake. He acted like I was one of his long lost buddies.

"Hey, Paco! What's up, man?"

"Not much," I lied.

"Is everything okay? We're good, right?" he asked.

"Yeah, we're good. It's just that I…" I didn't want to sound poor but I had to admit it. "I don't have a ticket and…"

"Oh, no problem. I got you covered," Trent said.

He leaned toward the ticket table, pulled out his wallet, and handed the lady a fifty. *Damn! What kind of 14 year-old walks around with his own posse and fifty dollar bills in his pocket? Answer: Trent Oden.* He patted me on the back and we all walked into the red-and-white-decorated gym together. It felt good to be with Trent's crew—even if they were only temporary, fake friends— because most of that day I had been completely alone.

Trent turned to me. "Paco, give me your cell number so I can text you with any changes in the plan."

It was embarrassing, but there was no avoiding it. "Uh, I don't have a cell phone."

"What?" he said in disbelief.

One of his friends in the crew laughed at me.

"Hey—" Trent got the guy's attention, "What are you laughing at, jackass? This guy's the key to our mission tonight."

The kid immediately stopped and turned his head in shame. It may have seemed like nothing from the outside, but it was a big deal. Trent had scolded and shut down a close friend to defend me. Trent was putting a lot of value on me. I guess it was his way of showing thanks and letting me know that he expected me to deliver. That and he was very serious about getting into Naomi's pants! He pulled me aside to speak in private.

"It's okay. We'll just go ahead as planned. 7:30 sharp," Trent said, like he was auditioning for a low-budget action movie. "That's in five minutes. Everyone will be in position in two. The emergency abort code word is 'Beyonce', OK?" I could tell he thought he was part James Bond part Jason Bourne.

"Understood," I said. "You've seen a lot of spy movies, huh?"

"What?" Trent said.

"Never mind, I'll just go with it," I said. Trent looked at me and then eyed my backpack with curiosity.

"Tequila," I said, anticipating his question.

He smiled. "Of, course! Nice job, Paco."

Of course? What the—? Just because I'm Mexican?

Trent exhaled and peered around the gym as it began to fill up.

"I have a feeling this is gonna be one helluva party," he said. "Come with me."

We sat in the bleachers, about 50 feet from the big refreshment table manned by one teacher and two kids on the student council. Trent knew that these goodie-goodies couldn't be trusted, and, of course, the teacher needed to be taken out of the equation, so he'd made arrangements.

At 7:28, a 7th grader they called 'Stinky' hobbled up to the refreshment table, doubled over, and complained of a horrible stomachache—Trent had paid him five dollars to do his best pathetic-sick-kid acting job. The teacher fell for it and led Stinky away from the table and out of the gym, headed toward the nurse's office. As they exited the building, two big 8th graders, Troy and Eric, approached the refreshment table and gently put their hands on the shoulders of the student council kids. Trent explained to me, in real time, that they were whispering into the kids' ears that the principal had requested their presence on the other side of campus. The gullible goodie-goodies exited the gym promptly, and Troy gave Trent the thumbs up from across the room. Trent nudged me with his elbow and said, "It's go time, Paco."

I tried to act natural as I walked down to the table now guarded by Trent's henchmen. I placed my backpack on the ground, grabbed the bottles and poured the Tequila into the huge punch bowl. It felt like it took five minutes to pour, but it was probably more like ten seconds. When I was done, the two henchmen smiled at me in approval. For the first time at Walden, I was part of something adventurous, rebellious, and cool. My adrenaline was pumping. I put the empty bottle in my bag and retreated back to base camp up on the bleachers. Trent was still there with his crew.

"Nice work, Paco," he said, giving me a fist bump. "The message is already out. The texts and posts are flying. Check it out."

I gazed down at the punch bowl area in disbelief. There was already a line thirty students long, with no teachers or chaperones in sight. The closest adults were across the gym, staring into their cell phones. The set up and execution of Operation Tequila Spike had gone down like clockwork.

Less predictable was what happened once the booze kicked in.

DANCING

The DJ turned up the music. Trent and his friends left me on the bleachers. He convinced me to wait where I was so I wouldn't get caught or raise any suspicions while they got in the spiked punch line. While I sat there by myself, something happened that had never happened before—a girl approached me.

She was tall and skinny, with dark black stringy hair and thick-rimmed glasses, wearing black jeans and a black sweater over a black tank top. She wasn't my type at all. Her skin looked like it hadn't seen the sun in years and she seemed nervous. She sat down next to me but didn't smile.

"Hi, I'm Nicol," she said.

"Hey, I'm Paco."

"I know," she said.

"Oh, are you candy-gram Nicol?" I asked.

"Yeah, I am."

"Oh, thanks for that," I said.

A wall of awkwardness seemed to be forming between us. Nicol obviously wanted to talk to me. Maybe she wanted to dance, maybe she wanted me to be her boyfriend. I didn't have much interest in her though. I was in love with Naomi and scanning the crowds and cliques scattered around the gym, trying to spot her. I began to see the irony of this cruel world—I wanted Naomi, but she was with Trent; Nicol wanted me, but I could care less about her. *Is this how Naomi felt about me?*

The DJ started pumping loud hip-hop (the censored versions) so it was hard to hear each other without shouting.

"What kind of music do you like?" she asked.

"Mostly old stuff," I said, "like Led Zeppelin, Rolling Stones, The Beatles."

"Ugh." She scrunched her face. "What about the Ramones?"

"Not so much," I said.

Our conversation pretty much went like that for another five minutes. Awkward silences, then her next question which would confirm the fact that we had nothing in common. At least she wasn't into Britney Spears and other cheesy pop music. I could tell she was reaching out to me, being nice in her own way, but I didn't really like her. The only thing I liked about Nicol was that she seemed to be interested in an innocent, selfless way—not because I knew a deep dark secret of hers or would help her get alcohol.

It was during our stunted, low-interest conversation that two guys approached us—Mitch and Omar—from Trent's secondary circle of friends.

"Hey Taco!" Mitch Potoroff yelled at me over the music, "I heard it was you, bro!"

I looked at him, confused at first, then I understood what "it" was. I didn't really want to announce that I was the Tequila guy, but it seemed the word was already out.

Omar laughed. "Yeah, we'll have to change your name from Taco to Senor Tequila!" he said.

He was the same guy who once called me "Dia de los Muertos." At that moment, I felt like my face was a painted on *calavera* (skull) mask. But instead of shame, it gave me strength.

"That's a good one," I said, "You should be proud of your originality and racist tendencies."

It was an aggressive comeback for me, but my attitude had shifted a bit—especially since I'd poured that Tequila into the punch bowl and knew I had Trent behind me. For the first time, I was a pivotal actor in the play, a major player in the game. Whatever it was that gave me temporary courage, it didn't matter. Omar probably didn't even hear me over the music (or get my sarcasm) because his response was, "Dude, glad you got this party started, bro!"

It made me uneasy. These guys knew I drugged the punch so it was only a matter of time before the entire school knew. *I should leave, run outside, and head home so I'll have an alibi.* As I was about to begin my escape, someone gently squeezed my shoulder. I assumed it was Nicol. But when I turned I was stunned by the image of a classic goddess with braided hair and a golden smile— Naomi Fox.

"Can I borrow you for a second?" she asked.

"Yes, please. I'm not a fan of these guys anyways," I said, leaning close to her ear so only she could hear me. I looked around and couldn't see candy-gram Nicol anywhere. She must have given up and fled. I felt kind of bad for neglecting her, but Naomi made me quickly forget my pinch of guilt.

Naomi walked me past the huge punch line and toward the dance area. When she paused at the edge of the dance floor and grabbed my hand, fear nailed me in the head like a dart. *I can't dance. And I especially can't dance with Trent's girlfriend!*

"What are we doing?" I said, terrified.

"Let's dance!" she said.

"Are you crazy? Do you want Trent to kill me?"

"Jeez, don't worry, Paco," she said, seductively close to my left ear. "He trusts a guy like you. Plus, he doesn't like to dance with me so it takes the pressure off him."

She smirked and stared into my eyes, which put me into a love-daze. Her neck tilted in dreamlike slow motion and her left hand extended out to me. She grabbed my wrist and dragged me onto the dance floor. She giggled and mouthed, "Come on, Paco."

I wasn't a good dancer. I wasn't even a decent dancer. Though I had no prior evidence, I'd describe myself as a horrible dancer. I had no interest in it and had no desire to get up in front of my classmates and shake my hips and wave my arms like I was really feeling the music. But there

I was, in the middle of the dance floor with Naomi Fox, bobbing my head, rolling my shoulders, and shifting my weight from side to side uncomfortably. I probably looked like a cross between Frankenstein and a nervous drug addict.

Naomi laughed sweetly. "Loosen up, Paco."

I tried to. I would do anything she told me to, really. I started to pick my feet off the ground and move my hands and arms more. I thought I was feeling the rhythm for a second and coming up with some pretty good moves until Naomi shouted, "Come on, Paco! You dance like my grandpa!"

Under normal circumstances her comment might have sent me running off the dance floor in tears, but not that day. Maybe it was the Tequila mission I'd just completed without a hitch, or the weird friendship I'd been building with her, but my confidence was up and it wasn't going to be destroyed by one discouraging dance comment. Plus, Naomi was still smiling.

The music shifted gears as a slow song started. No doubt about it. The song was super slow.

I inched away, preparing to flee the crowded dance area, but Naomi had different plans. "No, no, no, Paco," she said as she caressed my arm and pulled her body close to mine. Before I knew it, she'd wrapped one arm around my neck and the other around my waist.

"Slow songs are easy to dance to," she said. "Just follow me, side to side."

I was soon in heaven. Naomi was holding me, her head nestled close to my chest. She smelled like raspberry candy. It was probably perfume, but I wouldn't be surprised if she was born that way. And she was right: dancing to slow songs was easy—at least she made it seem easy. I got lost in the moment and the thought of spending the rest of my life with her, and that's when I felt Naomi's hand moving up my neck. Her fingers tickled my hair. It sent a euphoric sensation through my shoulders and up my spine.

Then reality hit. *She's gonna' get me killed!*

What if Trent saw her caressing me? Or one of his friends witnessed it and was just then telling Trent! Just dancing with Naomi on a slow song was a high-risk move. What was I thinking?

"Hey, Naomi, I think this is a bad idea," I said. "Trent's gonna' be pissed."

Naomi laughed, leaning into me as if she'd lost her balance. "Oh, don't be so paranoid. Trent's not as big and bad and power-mer-ful as he fronts." She giggled at herself and repeated, "Ha, I just said 'power-mer-ful'!"

When those last words came out of her mouth, Naomi was close enough to my nose to get a good whiff of her breath. The scent of fruity Tequila was heavy. I could have lit her last few words on fire. She stumbled, let out a shrieking laugh, and it was confirmed—Naomi was drunk.

She grabbed onto me and tried to keep on slow dancing, but it didn't feel the same.

When the song was over Naomi said, "Thanks for dancing with me, Paco. I have to go to the bathroom."

She twirled around, skipped off, and disappeared into the crowd.

I walked off the dance floor and looked back at the spot where we'd just been dancing. It was unreal. That's when someone patted me on the back and I turned to see Trent. *Damn.* I expected him to punch me in the face, or escort me to an isolated place away from any adults, and *then* punch me in the face.

"Hey, this party's going off, Paco! All thanks to you," Trent said. "Hey, have you seen Naomi?"

"Yeah, she just went to the bathroom," I said. I was afraid of what was coming next.

"Nice," he said, "Thanks for dancing with her and keeping her company while I was getting drinks and hanging with my crew."

What? Thanks?

"No problem," I said.

"Check that out!" Trent pointed to a puny 7th grade kid I didn't know.

Like half of the gym, we stood and stared as the kid projectile vomited a few feet away from the punch bowl. He was on one knee, regurgitating a pinkish mixture of punch, chips, Tequila, and who-knows-what-else. It was disgusting. The area around him cleared as more pink puke heaved from his mouth onto the hardwood floor. As people shouted and gawked, I noticed some of the other students were wobbly and loud. The Tequila had definitely kicked in.

The little puker yelled, "Oh, my god! What's happening to my body?"

All the onlookers laughed at this and some keeled over in hysterics. One redheaded 8th grade girl laughed so much that she started to vomit too. She grabbed her mouth as if she could stop the heaving process, then she bolted to the nearest trashcan. All hell was about to break loose.

"Cooooool. This is getting crazy," Trent said, "Well, I'm off to find my girlfriend." He winked as he lightly punched my shoulder. "Hopefully, the booze has loosened her up, bro."

He headed toward the girls' bathroom.

Damn. What a bastard. Trent was going to go take advantage of my sweet dream girl while she was drunk. It was now crystal clear that he'd planned the whole night for this very moment. He hadn't planned the alcohol for everyone else or for the sake of the party. It was all a ruse to get Naomi drunk so he could get around the virginity rule she'd laid down in the note.

Would I just stand there and let it happen?
Answer: No way.

It would be one thing if Naomi was sober and coherent, but she'd just been stumbling with me on the dance floor, caressing my neck, slurring her words. Trent would be doing something criminal if Naomi was too drunk to know any better. Yes, they were boyfriend and girlfriend, but—

she'd said it herself—she didn't want to lose her virginity before she was in high school. Now Trent was threatening her virtuous plan and maybe abusing his power.

Above all that magnanimous crap, I admit, I was jealous. The thought of them together killed me. I decided right then and there to stop Trent. How I would do it was still unclear as I left the chaos of the dance and went to save Naomi.

WHAT I SAW FROM BEHIND A DARK CURTAIN

The scene in the bathroom closest to the dance floor was surreal. There were a dozen kids shouting and cracking up, and some groaning in pain—complaining about spinning and nausea. Some were yelling the names of those who were already puking in the stalls. It was crazy. They were all wasted. At least thirty middle schoolers were overcome by alcohol for the first time in their lives and it was a true disaster. It was my fault, sure, but I wasn't too concerned about the drunken mobs or even the potential consequences.

I was too focused on finding Trent and saving Naomi. I guessed that Trent must have led her to a quiet, private place nearby. *But where?* Then it came to me—the performance theater. It was just down the hall and around the corner. The door was always open. It was dark. No one would suspect.

I jogged down the hall toward the theater and my brain caught up. *What was I going to do? Was I trying to save Naomi, or was I just jealous? What if Naomi changed her mind and wanted Trent to have sex with her and I interrupted them? I'd go from friend to enemy in a second, and then what? I'd be stuck between them in Mr. Holliday's class for the rest of the semester.*

No, none of that mattered. I had to do the right thing. Naomi was too drunk to make decisions and Trent was being too predatory. I had to stop him.

At the theater door, doubt made me hesitate again. I slowed my breathing and heard Naomi's voice inside. I opened the door slightly and quietly squeezed into the dark theater. I saw them kissing about thirty feet in front of me, right on the stage. Naomi wasn't exactly screaming for help. Trent was straddling her, but they were still fully clothed and he wasn't being forceful. I should have either stopped him or left right then—slipped out undetected. But, for some reason, I slid behind a dark curtain and watched.

Yes, peeping on them was slightly perverted. I'd gone from lovesick savior to wimpy creep-o in a second, but I was a curious teenage boy—give me a break! Seriously though, maybe I needed to see if Naomi really loved Trent, or if she was on the verge of rejecting him and I actually had a chance. Maybe she'd resist him and there'd be an opportunity to step in and stop Trent's advances at just the right time.

Or maybe the wiring in my brain was all screwed up.

Trent and Naomi didn't say a word for a minute. Their faces were locked in make-out city, but they were making faint moaning noises. I watched closely as Trent took off Naomi's shirt. The sight of her bare skin in only a bra and jeans was jaw dropping. *Damn.* I was in awe.

I stopped breathing for at least ten seconds. I couldn't believe what I was seeing. I would describe exactly what I saw, but that would be a bit crude. I have too much respect for Naomi—plus I still feel kind of guilty for peeping on them—so I will omit the details. I'll just say that I felt like I was secretly viewing a piece of fine art—one that belonged in a private collection where nobody (including me and Trent) could access. That image of Naomi laying supine on the stage will forever be imprinted in my memory.

I snapped out of my semi-perverted bliss when Trent stopped kissing her and reached for her belt. He unbuckled it and began to unbutton her pants. I was waiting, anxious, hoping that Naomi would stop him—a small, un-perverted confirmation that I loved her. And that's when it dawned on me and my internal voice spoke up: *Paco, the difference between love and lust is right in front of you. What's killing you is that Trent is making Naomi—a girl that you truly care for—nothing more than a sexual object. His lusting over Naomi's beauty is exactly what's making him blind to her depth, her intelligence, her wishes. It's what makes him a jerk, Paco! Don't go down that same road, man. Now's your chance to protect Naomi and prove your love. Put an end to this!*

I was just about to bolt onto the stage when I heard her voice.

"Wait, Trent!" Naomi grabbed the waistline of her pants and pulled them up. "I told you, I don't want to do this yet."

"It's okay, baby," he said, "I love you."

Ughhh. That bastard.

"Do you really?" she asked.

"Yeah, I do," he said, as he reached to pull her pants down again.

"Then, you'll wait," she said, shifting away from him, "If you love me you'll wait."

Trent would've tried again and again if Naomi hadn't kept talking in a tone that was so obviously disapproving. She seemed to be expecting a halfway sensitive, decent response, but she got only a blank stare from him.

"If you really love someone, then you respect them," she said. "You respect me."

As I watched from behind that musty curtain, I could see that I didn't need to "save" Naomi. She was doing a much better job of saving herself.

"Do you love me?" Trent asked.

It may have been the first vulnerable thing I'd ever heard Trent say.

Naomi hesitated, clearly uncomfortable. Silent, she covered herself up with her hands.

That's when the theater doors burst open and in came Mr. Holliday with the huge Tequila punch bowl cradled in his arms. Surprised by his abrupt entry, Naomi shrieked.

I hid and cowered behind the curtain, praying no one could see me.

Mr. Holliday stared in disbelief at the two on stage.

"What the heck is going on here?" he said.

"Sorry, Mr. Holliday," Trent pleaded, sounding like a frog got caught in his throat, "We were just—

"Are you kidding me?" Holliday interrupted, "There's no excuse for you two being in here alone. Get your clothes on young lady and you, Trent..."

It seemed that Mr. Holliday was momentarily at a loss for words. He must have been tasked with getting rid of the Tequila punchbowl after bearing witness to the mess in the gym, and now this: Trent on top of Naomi, half-undressed, on the theater stage!

"Trent, come out into the hall," he said. "You too, missy!"

He pointed at a shamed, yet still intoxicated Naomi. She looked like a deer caught in headlights—a semi-drunk but quickly sobering deer. Still, a gorgeous deer who had just fended off a wolf.

I crouched there behind the curtain, motionless, trying to breathe quietly as the couple moved from the stage to the exit. Once Trent and Naomi were by the door, Mr. Holliday stood toe-to-toe with them.

"I'd ask, but I don't even think I want to know," he said.

Trent and Naomi didn't say a word. They appeared to be more embarrassed than frightened.

"You two are in big trouble," Mr. Holliday scolded them. "You need to go straight to the office right now. The main secretary will be waiting for you and that's where your parents will have to pick you up."

I heard footsteps walking away and let out a sigh, assuming Mr. Holliday was escorting the couple. But

Holliday came back inside and closed the door. I froze, hoping he wouldn't turn on the lights.

"You gotta' be kidding me," he said out loud, unaware that anyone else was in the room. He stood by the nearly empty punchbowl and grabbed a small plastic cup that was floating inside. From what I could hear, he dipped it in, filled the cup, and drank down my special Tequila mixture all in one gulp. He paused and grunted in approval as if to say, "Not bad," then swigged another cupful before he went out the door.

I must have waited a full five, maybe ten, minutes before I moved from behind that curtain, afraid that someone else—teacher or student—might come in. Finally, I peeked out into the hallway and didn't see anyone. I ran as fast as I could to the back of the school, jumped the fence, and kept running almost all the way home.

PRINCIPAL'S OFFICE

The next morning, before I'd even walked through the front doors of the school, I knew it would be a rough day. At best, by some miracle, I wouldn't be blamed for the drunken chaos the night before, but would still worry all day about the possibility of getting caught. At that point, I thought there was a slim chance I might get away with the whole Tequila incident scot-free.

As I walked through the halls toward my locker, I heard murmuring around me from students I didn't know.

"There's Taco," someone said.

"Senor Tequila now," said another guy.

"Maybe he'll get expelled."

"Probably."

After 30 seconds of passing through cliques of my peers and hearing random comments about the dance and my grim future, I was scared. It was much worse than I thought. I noticed Nicol, the Ramones-candy-gram girl, leaning next to my locker as I approached it. She looked even less interesting than she had the night before.

"I hate you," she said.

"What?"

"I'm just joking!" Nicol said, "But you got me drunk last night and, aside from the first hour, it wasn't very fun."

"I got you drunk?" I asked.

"Save it, Paco. Everybody knows it was you."

"Seriously? How?"

"I don't know, but they've already given you a new name: 'Senor Tequila.'"

Damn. I stood there in disbelief, wanting to run out the front entrance and never come back. I wanted to transfer districts. Then I realized that I might not have a choice—I might be expelled from Walden.

Even though she kind of annoyed me, I appreciated that Nicol took it upon herself to update me about Trent and Naomi. According to her, they had to wait in the office until 10pm, when their parents came to pick them up. At one point Trent cried. And right after that Naomi puked on his leg. They were both suspended for the day. Maybe, I thought, it could be the beginning of the end of their relationship.

Even amidst my imminent doom, that was some pretty good news.

I smiled at Nicol and thanked her for the information, then felt a friendly pat on the back from a passerby. "Way to go, Paco!" a big 8th grader named James Malone told me. "Last night was awesome, dude."

...

I'd been sitting in science class for maybe five minutes of the first period—observing the curious stares of my classmates, hearing whispers and gestures in my direction, feeling the wrong kind of popularity—when someone hand-delivered a note to my teacher.

"Paco Jones," my teacher said, "You need to report to the office immediately."

I felt like a 'dead man walking' through those empty halls all the way to the office. Everyone was in class. I was all alone.

I imagined I'd be talking to the vice principal or the dean, two people I'd only seen at monthly assemblies. Though it would be new to me, the idea of getting in trouble at school wasn't nearly as frightening as facing my father. He didn't take kindly to behavioral missteps— anything that could be construed as disrespecting him or shaming our family. And he reserved a special kind of anger for mistakes that cost him time (away from work or his TV sports viewing) or money (the thousands in tuition he'd been sacrificing for my education). I still held out hope that he'd never hear about the Tequila incident, but I couldn't imagine getting busted and the office not calling my parents.

As soon as I entered the front office, they were ready for me. The matronly secretary led me to the faded blue door labeled "Principal's Office."

Principal's office? This is serious.

The secretary opened the door and led me to a dark brown leather seat facing his desk. He was on the phone, facing the window. The room looked kind of like a doctor's office, with framed degrees and awards on the walls.

There was a placard on the desk that read, "Dr. Bennett." When the secretary left the room and I sat down, he motioned for me to wait. I had only seen him a few times on campus. He seemed like a nice man, about fifty years old, with mostly gray hair. His hairline receded so much that it looked like his forehead was never-ending. He had on a light brown, outdated suit and a thick dark brown tie.

Dr. Bennett spoke to the person on the other end of that phone with a real sense of purpose. He hadn't even looked at me yet because he was so focused on whatever business that phone call was about. When he hung up the phone, however, he swiveled his chair and turned his intense stare and attention directly at me.

"You're Mr. Jones, is that correct?" he said.

"Yes, Paco," I said.

"Mr. Jones do you have any idea why you're here in my office?" he asked. His tone was austere, his expression deadpan. This guy's presence was unreal—like Agent Smith interrogating Neo in *The Matrix*. But he didn't make me feel like a criminal, didn't talk down to me like most other adults would. Dr. Bennett spoke to me with a scary amount of *respect*.

"No, I'm not exactly sure," I lied.

"Not exactly sure?" he repeated, "Well, Mr. Jones, I'm not necessarily asking you to recount every detail with precision or accuracy. Nor am I asking you to recall events—that may or may not incriminate you—with the certitude of a post-doctoral scholar."

What? It was too intense. This guy didn't mess around. *What had he just said?*

"I'm asking you if you have any idea why you are here because if you do have an idea— a modicum of knowledge—and you refuse to disclose crucial information upfront, yet the truth about your guilt in the matter emerges later, then the consequences for you, Mr. Jones, will be grave. Do you understand me?"

"Um, not really," I said.

"In other words, Mr. Jones," he warned, "You should tell me the whole truth right now."

I was terrified, almost shaking. I couldn't see myself pleading the fifth, keeping my mouth shut, and getting away with it. Dr. Bennett was too sharp, too intelligent. I'd only been sitting in front of him for a minute and I was ready to crack.

"Well…" I stalled.

A few seconds passed.

"Mr. Jones?"

"Is this about the Tequila?" I said.

"You're on the right track, Mr. Jones," he said. "Please continue."

I told him the whole story. Well, not the entire story. I told him my part. Though I considered throwing Trent and some of his friends under the bus, I figured it was not a good way to win friends or Naomi's affection. So I did the noble thing—I took almost all the blame. I told Dr. Bennett that "Operation Tequila Spike" was my plan, and that I did it to make the dance more fun and to impress people. I told him I worked alone; that I barely had any friends at school anyway. At least the last part was true.

"You're sure nobody put you up to this, Mr. Jones?" Dr. Bennett asked.

"Nobody."

"And there aren't any details you're leaving out that I should know about?"

I thought about the moment Trent asked me to bring alcohol; what I'd seen of Trent and Naomi on stage, kissing; Mr. Holliday taking those two big swigs of Tequila punch.

"No, nothing else."

"May I ask you, Mr. Jones," Dr. Bennett said, "Why Tequila?"

I could have sworn that Dr. Bennett had a smirk on his face for a split second, just as the word "Tequila" left his mouth.

"Honestly," I said, "It was the only full bottle of liquor in my parent's house."

"I see."

"Dr. Bennett," I said shakily, "Are you going to tell them?"

"Of course," he said, "They'll be notified by phone later today."

My chest sunk. My heart shrunk. Five internal "*Damns*" weren't enough to express my devastation. Normal time turned to slow motion with the gravity of this news.

———

I pictured my mom crying, my father fuming—boiling. It was hard to swallow, literally, but Dr. Bennett was not finished, and he took another direction.

"Mr. Jones, is it true that your classmates have called you 'Taco' in a derogatory fashion?"

"Yes," I said. I saw no reason to lie.

"And there are now reports of some calling you Senor Tequila," he added.

"Yeah."

"Does this kind of racial discrimination happen often at this school?"

He was dead serious.

"It happens sometimes."

"And how do you handle it?"

"I try to ignore it," I said. "My mom tells me that the type of people who say that stuff are ignorant anyways."

"Ignore the ignorant," he said, "Not a bad motto, Mr. Jones. Your mother is smart."

"Not the best motto for those in the field of education though," I said. It was risky, but I felt that Dr. Bennett would appreciate my humor.

"Ha. You're right, Mr. Jones. Very clever," he said. "I would think your grades would more accurately reflect your apparent intelligence, but unfortunately they don't."

"You're right," I admitted. *Touché.*

"Do you ever feel angry during or after school?" he asked.

"No, not really," I said.

"So you don't seek any form of revenge?—Or escape?"

"No, Dr. Bennett."

"Did you know, Mr. Jones, that almost twenty-five percent of Latino students drop out of school by 8th grade?"

"No, sir," I said.

"Do you want to be in this school, Mr. Jones?" he asked.

"Yes," I said. It was a frightening line of questioning. *Was he going to expel me?*

"Do you know that your education is crucial for your success?"

"Yes."

"Do you like history, Mr. Jones?" Dr. Bennett asked.

"Yeah, a little bit," I said. *Why*?

He paused, stood up from his desk, and walked over to a cabinet that held a large jar of jellybeans. While standing up, it was clear that Dr. Bennett was short. He was shorter than me, yet his personality and intellect felt larger than the room. I had no idea what was coming next.

Dr. Bennett asked: "Have you ever heard of General Antonio Lopez de Santa Anna?"

"No," I said.

"He was a famous Mexican leader who made infamous errors throughout his career, Mr. Jones." Dr. Bennett paused. "He started off his career as a brilliant military general and revolutionary president, but he died in pathetic obscurity, disabled, nearly blind, barely allowed back into his native country. When Santa Anna's rightful time to lead was over, he wouldn't accept it. He forced his way back into power, killed innocents, and corrupted himself in the most heinous ways. Because of this he was repeatedly exiled, imprisoned, shot, crippled, and disgraced."

Dr. Bennett took a step forward, closing the space between us.

"This point is crucial, Mr. Jones—Santa Anna had great potential, and had some great success, but he made the same mistakes over and over again. He never learned from those mistakes... His selfishness and his ego always got in the way."

I nodded, trying to focus and understand his words. Despite the punitive lecture, I liked that Dr. Bennett didn't speak to me in a condescending way, like I was some dumb kid. Instead, he made me feel like I was the lone student in his university history course.

"... You've made some mistakes, Mr. Jones," he said. "We need not review all the critical details, but you've made several mistakes and you're aware of the severe liabilities you've placed on the school in the process. The legal implications are huge. Your errors in judgment harmed other students and could have been disastrous for them and their families."

His delivery sounded intimidating and polished, as if it was a prepared speech.

"However, Mr. Jones, you've done the right thing in surrendering crucial information and making this process relatively smooth. You'll be allowed to stay in this school and further your education here because I sincerely think this institution is the best chance you have... Do not squander that chance, Mr. Jones. Do not make the same mistakes again. I'm betting on your potential. As you focus on educating yourself and searching for truth in this world, those ignorant individuals who call you names will become less and less significant in your life. But if you do experience more racism here at Walden, please tell me or another teacher. I've spent a good portion of my life fighting against injustice and I don't intend to stop now. Do you understand me, Mr. Jones?"

His speech had me on the verge of tears. But if I cried it would be half because of his touching, thoughtful speech, and half from my fear of the forthcoming pain and misery I faced from my parents.

He continued, "I have faith in you, Mr. Jones, but, regardless, there have to be consequences."

Seconds later I walked out of his office trying to wrap my head around the consequences: Two days of in-school suspension, three consecutive weeks of after-school detention, and probation for the rest of the school year. If I screwed up again, I'd be expelled.

When I got home that afternoon I snuck into my room and checked my FriendMe account. I had 37 messages and 122 new friend requests. Before I could read any of them, my mom came into my room and took the computer.

"You're on restriction for a long time, mijo," she said with a solemn expression.

It began immediately—an in-house restriction that was based on a complete cut off from technology and the outside world. No screens whatsoever. Anything that required plugging in or charging was removed from my room.

"Ay, dios mio," she said. "I'm very disappointed in you."

"Sorry, mom."

"Sorry is not enough, mijo," she said. "Wait till your father hears about this."

And that's exactly what I was most afraid of—my father.

Later that night, he came into my bedroom. Before he'd said a single word to me, I could see the indignation in his eyes. His body language—anxiously shifting and taking deep breaths—made it look as if he was about to explode. His intense, angry silence made me nearly pee my pants. For a second, I thought he might hit me, but he wasn't the abusive type. At first he spoke with an eerie calm about how I had disrespected myself and my family, then he reeled off a list of all the things I had done wrong.

It didn't take long for me to start bawling. While I cried, he raised his voice, yelling at me about wasting his time and money. He warned me to never mess up again, or he'd pull me out of Walden and send me to the worst public school in the area—Hoover Junior High—where kids got bullied and robbed daily, and sometimes even stabbed and shot.

I got the message.

After he left my room I kept crying—but not from any physical pain. Physical pain was nothing compared to the heavy guilt that now weighed on me.

I kept crying because I'd shamed my entire family.

CRIME AND PUNISHMENT

When I returned from school every day, I was confined to my computer-less, music-less, phone-less room. The only thing I could do was my homework, read, or draw. *Damn. Medieval times*! I left my cell only to eat breakfast and dinner, and bathe. Yes, I started calling my bedroom "my cell" because that's exactly what it felt like—a jail cell. But I only said it under my breath or in private because I didn't want the wardens to increase my sentence for bad behavior. It was like practicing for prison life.

Because of the tone they'd set, I was mostly quiet with my parents during my restriction. My dad didn't speak to me for the first week, and when he finally tried to be kind enough to utter a few words in my direction, I had no interest in speaking back to him. I'd give him a semi-polite "yes" or "no," or a head nod. I resented that he'd taken a harsher, more primitive, and more punitive stance with me than Dr. Bennett had—some administrator guy that wasn't even related by blood. My mom gave me the silent treatment on and off, but I could tell that she was concerned about me. She paid more attention to my moods, and asked questions about how I was doing and how life was at school. I think she was concerned about her *mijito*, her baby. She didn't want me to turn into a criminal.

Using the word "criminal" might sound a bit extreme, but it's surprising what kind of adult response can emerge from one illegal teenage act.

Sometimes, when I was unresponsive to either of my parents at the dining room table, they'd give me a look that I'd never seen before. They'd stare at me as if they knew me well, but at the same time were afraid that I might turn into a monster at any minute, as if I might wake up the next morning as Frankenstein, or some alien species might take over my brain and turn me into a vicious thug. It made me realize how influential—and how vulnerable—my parents were. *What if they started to treat me differently—like a criminal—because I'd gotten in trouble at school? Would I eventually start to act like one? Would I rebel and become a thug?*

After seeing a glimpse of the thug life, I didn't want to become one—despite the momentary fame it brought me at school.

ALMOST FAMOUS

The three weeks of detention at school weren't much of a punishment compared to my home life in a Mexican-American prison cell.

No, detention at school wasn't bad at all.

It was just boring—and a bit depressing.

It consisted of reporting to the same colorless, paint-smelling room every day during recess and after school for forty-five minutes. A rotation of teachers (maybe those who were also being punished by the principal) would be stationed at the desk. There would be directions on the board: clean up duties, a mindless repetitive writing task, or directions to "read a book"—as if that wasn't an ironic punishment for an educator to dish out.

I didn't fit into the detention crowd and I didn't want to. The regulars there were like regular drunks at a local pub. They migrated into the barren detention room as if by force of habit. I was at least expecting to hear some good jokes, or stories about their wayward law-breaking, but the group was usually sedate. They didn't talk much or cause many disturbances. Their form of defiance was to sleep, or to do nothing at all. For the most part, it was a big waste of time.

Time that would have been better spent talking to Naomi.

Time that I could have spent soaking up my new popularity.

Oh, I haven't mentioned that yet?

Less than twenty-four hours after the dance ended and my punishment began, news of my sole responsibility for the debauchery at the Valentine's dance spread fast. In the halls and through the cliques on campus, all over FriendMe and PostPics, the drunken Tequila debacle became known as "The Famous Tequila Incident" almost overnight.

Any moment that I wasn't in the middle of class or in detention, my fellow students gave me tons of attention. Sometimes they just turned toward me in the halls—whole groups at a time—nodding, saying "What's up?" or giving me the thumbs up. Some handed me personal notes: *Viva Tequila! You rock, Paco! When's the next party?* and *You're FriendMe Famous, bro!'*

The "FriendMe Famous" comments referred to the wildly popular event page some students had created and named "The Famous Tequila Incident" which had tons of pictures from that infamous night. It glorified and lionized me. Teachers had no idea it existed. Random students patted me on the back in passing. They gave me high fives in the halls for no apparent reason. Some people approached me and wanted to know more details—and what my next prank would be. They wanted to talk to me, Senor Tequila. That's what they started to call me, as if it signified my new, higher rank in the army of adolescent dumbasses who were trying to define what was cool and what was not.

And that was the thing: It didn't make any sense. Before all this, I wasn't cool at all. I was just the Mexican kid with a funny name. Now my classmates were looking to me for the next cool thing! These were the same people that could care less about me the week before, that didn't look in my direction or give me the slightest expression of acknowledging my existence—unless they were making fun of my Mexican-ness.

During that first week of faux-fame, after Mr. Holliday's class, on my way to detention, Trent strolled up next to me and put his hand on my shoulder.

"Hey Pac, what's up?"

"Not much," I said, "Just going to do my time."

"Yeah, about that," he said, "You really stepped up, man."

"What are you talking about?"

Trent looked around the halls as if he was afraid we were under surveillance.

"You didn't snitch, bro. That takes some balls," he said. "You could have had me and my crew crucified. Bennett might have expelled me."

"No problem," I said. *I'm not a snitch, I thought, but would I have snitched if it meant Trent being expelled, thus clearing the way to Naomi? Probably!*

"I owe you, man," Trent said.

"No, you don't."

But before I could turn and continue on to the detention room, Trent pulled his hand out of his pocket and slapped a fifty-dollar bill in my right hand.

"This is for the Tequila and the party of the decade, Paco."

One might think that so much attention and approval from fellow junior high classmates would be a welcomed development, but there was a problem with it.

I was uncomfortable with my new "friends"—mostly because they weren't really my friends at all. I was "trending" but it wasn't for having done anything I was proud of or that was worthy of idolizing. And being "FriendMe Famous" was as phony and fake as it sounded. In fact, it was kind of scary. Because of one ill-planned event—that was captured on camera phones, video, and retold on post after post—I had been blasted into popularity. *But was that why I'd done it? Was that why I'd stolen the booze, spiked the punch, gotten everyone drunk, and took all the blame?*

No.

In a strange and illogical way, I had done it all for Naomi.

Any pressure I'd felt from Trent and his crew was compounded because of Naomi.

Any pressure I had put on myself that night, or desire to be cool, was because of Naomi.

As impossible at it seemed, I was willing to do anything for her.

So what did she think of Senor Tequila?

I had no idea because during the first week after the Famous Tequila Incident, I was on restriction and too scared to talk to her. I feared that if I spoke to her, looked straight into her eyes, she'd sense that I had seen her half-naked on the stage with Trent. I was afraid that she'd think the whole Tequila debacle was idiotic, immature, and my fault. And I was afraid that—after having that close-up, intimate dance with her—Trent would get word of it and suspect me of trying to put the moves on his beloved girlfriend if I tried to get close to her again.

The second week after the Famous Tequila Incident, Naomi was on vacation.

She wasn't at school the whole week.

Trent told me she was "overseas."

At the time I wasn't exactly sure what that meant, but assumed it meant that she was very, very far away.

MOVIE MIRACLE

Toward the tail end of my probationary house arrest, my parental units began to show signs of guilt for giving me the medieval dungeon treatment for so long. Though they didn't say this, or go so far as give my computer back early, they did start acting much nicer and more talkative than usual. Then—when I emerged from my cell for an early dinner on the second to last day of my restriction—their tone completely changed.

"How are you, mijo?" my mom asked.

"I'm okay," I said.

"It must be tough, Paco," my dad said.

"What do you mean?" I said.

"I mean being on restriction," he said. "You've been suffering at school *and* here at home, and it must be tough."

It sounded like my dad's way of attempting to connect to me—to my suffering. The problem was that he was the one who was causing my suffering.

"You've done a good job," he added.

Done a good job? How does one do a good job of being punished? When my alternatives are intense parental guilt trips or more days of penitentiary-type restriction, then good behavior was really my only logical option. What the hell was my dad talking about?

Of course, I didn't respond out loud because I didn't know what to say.

"Paco, don't you have anything to say?" my dad added, his short-lived empathy seemed to be disappearing fast.

"Don't be pushy, Paul," my mom said.

"Maria, I am not being pushy," he said, with an undercurrent of discomfort, "I'm trying to relate here and let Paco know that I'm..."

It seemed like he was about to say "sorry," but that would've been an all-time first for my dad and—as if the word had caught his tongue—he knew it, too.

"... That, eh, his punishment is over," he finished.

"Almost over," my mom corrected.

Wait, was she on my side or not?

"No, I think he's had enough, honey," he said.

My mom and dad exchanged odd parental glances, which hinted that they'd recently discussed having this conversation with me, yet they had never come to a final decision on the details of ending my punishment early. Thus, the confused look on my mom's face.

"Really?" I asked. "It's over?"

"The key question is..." my dad said, "Do you understand why we were so upset with you?"

"Yeah," I said, "I mean, drinking's illegal for kids, I stole from you guys and I almost got expelled from school."

"No," my dad said, "I mean, yes, those are all reasons, but there's a bigger one."

"What are you talking about?"

My dad looked at my mom and then back at me.

"You're not like most of the kids at your school," he said.

"You mean white?" I asked.

My mom laughed.

"No, don't be silly. *I'm* white," he said. "I mean rich. The kids at Walden are rich, Paco, and we're not rich. Those kids can screw around, get in trouble, get bad grades, and then their parents can bail them out, like George Bush. They have money, but we can't afford to do that."

"Is this all about money?" I asked, looking at my food, losing my appetite.

"No, mijo," my mom chimed in.

"Paco, it's about your education," my dad said. "You can't waste it. It's your shot at being successful in this world."

"Well, you could have just told me that," I said.

"I am telling you now," he said, and glanced over at my mom. "We're telling you this because we care about you."

It wasn't an apology for giving me the shaming dungeon treatment, but it was as close as my dad was going to get.

"Paco," my mom said, "Do you want to come to the movies with us tonight?"

"Um, I don't know."

"It's the latest Jason Bourne movie," my dad added. "I think you'll like it."

It was a gesture, an awkward one, but it was a nice gesture—like my parents' version of an Indian peace pipe.

"Okay," I said.

The shift in my parents' disciplinary angle took a few hours for me to process. It was as if they'd seen me harden over the weeks and didn't want me to turn into a full on criminal. But I don't know. Parents can be strange. I'm guessing they—prompted by my mom—started to blame themselves for my misbehavior. Maybe they felt guilty for being too harsh, or guilt for something else? After all, they were technically Catholic. And it had been years since my dad and I had done any of the father-son things we used to do when I was a kid, like play catch, ride bikes to the beach, and go to the movies. I suppose when kids hit puberty, parents begin to feel like it's better to keep their distance...so they do.

But really, who knows?

By the time we sat in our plush movie theater seats, I found I wasn't looking forward to Jason Bourne. I'd loved the first Bourne film—the international locations, the intense fight scenes, and Bourne's impossible multi-lingualism—but that night I could care less about any of that. Instead I imagined life after punishment, projecting dream-like visions of being with Naomi—her eyes, her smooth brown skin, the smell of her hair; her hand stroking my neck during that slow dance; chatting with her about non-cheesy music like we had that first time; talking to her about Romeo and Juliet like we had in class; listening to her sharp psychoanalysis.

But how would I re-enter her life?

Pass her a note in Mr. Holliday's class?

Send her a lame message on FriendMe?

And what would it say?—*Missed you while you were gone and I was cut off from the world for three weeks. By the way, I'm madly in love with you, so please break up with Trent and be with me. Sincerely, Paco*?

There were at least three problems with this scenario: 1) It didn't seem likely that I'd have the courage to write anything expressive and honest to Naomi. But if I did, then 2) Trent might find out and get pissed off and kill me, and 3) It didn't seem likely that Naomi would ever break up with Trent to be with me anyway.

Not a chance, actually.

As the first movie preview boomed onto the screen, I got up to go to the bathroom. My mom looked at me and I mouthed the word "bathroom" to clarify that I wasn't trying to escape or abuse my new freedom. She nodded back to me and I walked up the aisle, picturing Naomi's smile and how to navigate that middle ground between my obsession and my reality.

In the wide hallway, just after I spotted the entrance to the restroom, I heard a voice—a wonderful, transcendent voice.

"Hey, Paco!" she said.

It was Naomi. She was holding a bag of buttered popcorn and a Coke.

"Hi," I said—surprised. No, I was dumbfounded. *What were the chances?*

Naomi smiled and hugged me as if we were long lost friends. It was a warm, extended hug that sent a flood of endorphins through my body like a river of happiness. I couldn't believe it. She pulled back and looked me in the eyes.

"Are you okay, Paco?"

"Yeah. I'm good, thanks," I said. "You?"

"I'm pretty good," she said.

I didn't know what to say. I wanted to confess my undying love to her right then and there. It was the only thing running through my mind: *I love you, I love you, I love you*. Just like in that Beatles song "Michelle." But I kept it in. I figured it would catch her off guard and freak her out.

"How was your trip?" I asked, knowing I had to say something to avoid a really awkward silence.

"It was okay," she said, shrugging. "Sofia is kind of a weird place."

Sofia? I had no idea where in the world Sofia was located. Was it a country, a city, an island? I didn't want to sound stupid, so I didn't ask. I didn't have to.

"I gave you that extra big hug because I know," she said. "I know."

She smirked and tilted her head to the side in that cute—no, gorgeous—way only Naomi could pull off. I was lost in the beauty of her gaze for a moment before the fear hit me.

What did she know?

That I was dumb and had no idea where Sofia was?

That I saw her half-naked in the theater?

That I was madly in love with her?

"What do you know?" I asked.

"I know that Trent isn't bright or sweet enough to have come up with my Valentine's Day present by himself," she said. "I know that he came to you because he's clueless and that you consulted him. He admitted it when I called him on it."

"Oh," I said.

I didn't know if she considered this discovery a good or a bad thing.

"And I assume that you sent me those anonymous candy-grams, right?"

"Yeah, you got me," I said. My insides trembled.

"That was sweet of you," she said with a big smile that lit up the dark maroon-carpeted hallway.

"Thanks," I said. I smiled so big and wide I felt goofy. A tingly sensation ran through me. "I'm just glad you didn't think it was creepy."

"No, not at all," Naomi said, "But you know who's been creeping me out lately?"

"Who?"

"Trent."

I almost blurted out a laugh of joy and celebration, but instead—in stopping myself—let out a very weird, failed trumpet-sounding noise from my nose.

"Are you okay?" she asked.

"Yeah," I said.

I needed to play it cool, or at least try to. If my intuitions were correct, she trusted me more than I ever imagined a girl of her caliber trusting a guy like me and I couldn't ruin it now.

"Anyways," she said, "Trent's been acting strange recently. Like when he got angry at some 7th grade boy who was looking at me as we passed him in the hall. Trent pushed the little guy and knocked him down, but for what? For looking in my direction? He's done it a lot lately—being all defensive and violent."

Naomi went on to describe Trent's recent behavior— angry, nervous and uptight. She mentioned that he'd started asking her dumb racial questions.

"He'll ask me things like 'Do you like white guys more than black guys?' or 'Am I good enough for you, or am I too white?' and 'Do you promise to stay with me no matter what, or are you just in a white-guy phase?'"

Aside from the paranoid racial views he'd been exposing, she said Trent had also been revealing a new level of insecurity and lack of confidence that she described as "repulsive."

I have to admit, as bad as it may sound, hearing this was music to my ears. And it gave me some insight on what kind of attitudes girls considered attractive—or not.

"Really?" I said. *Please, tell me more about how disgusted you are with Trent Oden.*

"And," Naomi added, "Now that I know about your romantic behind-the-scenes role, I want you to know how refreshing your paraphrasing of Romeo and Juliet was to my heart and soul, Paco. When I read it, I instantly knew that you—a unique ship in a sea of moronic boys—were the writer. No way Trent could've done that."

"Thanks," I said, and then summoned the courage to say, "Well, I meant it."

"Meant what?" she asked.

"Um," I balked. Apparently, courage had slipped out the emergency exit door. "I don't know—the words?"

Naomi smiled. "You're so cute, Paco."

She reached out and ran her fingers through my hair and said, "Cool hair." It was the best sensation, even though I didn't believe that my messy mop was anything near cool.

"Cool hair"—that was Naomi's parting comment before she gracefully spun around and skipped back to her movie theater.

HOOPS

Under normal circumstances, I wouldn't have been able to stay on the basketball team after the Famous Tequila Incident and weeks of detention. However, two things kept me on the team: 1) My dad emailed the principal and the coach and—because my dad was so convinced that playing a sport would be good for me—pleaded on my behalf so I could remain on the team; 2) Due to progress reports being issued that week, five players (three of them starters) had been disqualified for having failing grades. This left Coach Huskie in a bit of a predicament. With only eight eligible players left on the roster, he couldn't afford to lose another player, even if I was the last option on the bench. Still, I wasn't allowed to practice until my restriction was over—which happened to be the day after I miraculously ran into Naomi at the movies.

I assumed it would be strange to re-enter the basketball team after weeks of not practicing. I was already one of the worst on the team. And I was afraid the other players would resent me for not working, suffering, and sweating alongside them, but that wasn't the case. Instead of getting flack, I got praise. Apparently my campus celebrity status had followed me into the locker room. Middle schoolers didn't make any sense whatsoever.

"Out on good behavior?" said Alan Jacobsen, the second best player on the team who had never talked to me before.

"Yeah, I guess," I said.

A few of the players laughed as they laced up their hundred-dollar Nikes.

"Just remember to invite us to the next Tequila party, eh," Mitch said.

"Paco, you get any tattoos while you were in prison?" Alan asked.

"Nope," I said.

"Maybe your game will be tougher now," Ryan, the freckly kid, said.

"Yeah, maybe," I replied.

That's when Trent, who'd been uncharacteristically quiet, chimed in: "Paco's building confidence. That's big. Isn't it, Paco?"

"Yeah," I said, worried about what Trent knew and what he meant by that. Did he think I was over stepping my bounds, getting too close to (too confident with) his girlfriend—whom he was insecurely grasping onto? Or was I being paranoid?

"Well, let's go play some ball then, Mr. Confidence," Alan said.

A couple of the guys laughed again, but this time I knew it was because they viewed me as the worst player on the team and expected me to remain nothing more than that.

What my fellow teammates didn't know was that one of the books I'd read during my restriction in a Mexican-American prison cell was by the famous UCLA basketball coach John Wooden. I didn't know if my dad had strategically left it out for me, but once I started reading it I couldn't put it down. I read it in two days and, though there were many pieces of practical advice on team sports and life in general, I really remembered this one quote from Wooden: "Try your best to be the best that you can be, and you will feel good about your efforts, regardless of the outcome." It might have sounded like "loser advice" if it hadn't come from John Wooden—the biggest winner in the history of college sports.

When we lined up on the baseline of the court, Coach Huskie shouted at us—as always—to stand up straight with our feet behind the painted line.

"You know what to do, gentlemen," he said, then placed the whistle in his mouth.

He blew it hard and loud.

We darted from the baseline to half court, then back to the baseline, then sprinted the full length of the court and back.

Suicides.

We usually started and ended practice with this type of torturous running, and sometimes it was the only part of practice that I remembered. Our team didn't focus much on offensive strategy or defensive technique, but we sure ran a lot. Trent always finished first because he was the fastest at suicides.

Later on in practice, while we were hustling through shooting drills, I realized that Mr. Wooden's advice would only come in handy if I tried my best in the best way possible. So, rather than shooting the way I usually shot the ball—heaving it toward the basket with no particular style and praying it would go in—I studied the best shooters on the team: Alan and Trent. I noticed how they squared their feet to face the basket, bent their elbows, used the off hand to guide the ball, and snapped their wrists as they released.

I tried this over and over until it felt almost natural. *Shoot to make it.*

After a few minutes, I was actually making some shots and Alan noticed, too.

"Nice shot, Paco," he said.

Maybe reading books could help me more than I'd thought. After all, books did help out with Naomi—it was the Romeo and Juliet lines that really earned me some points. At least that's what she'd told me.

Once Naomi had crossed my mind, I couldn't help but glance at Trent out on the court and remember what she'd said about him. He'd just driven to the basket hard and nailed some kid in the face with his elbow on the way in. Coach called an offensive foul on Trent.

"What? That was nothing!" Trent yelled.

It was uncharacteristic. Trent never talked back to our coach.

"Don't argue with the ref," Coach said.

"You gotta be fricking kidding me!" Trent shot back.

"Trent!" Coach barked, "Calm down or you'll be running the rest of practice."

"Fine," Trent said.

But Trent wasn't fine. He'd been scowling and quiet since the beginning of practice. He was usually the center of attention in the locker room before practice, but he hadn't said more than his single comment about my confidence. He gave no side comments or head nods on the court either. This was unusual considering that ever since the Famous Tequila Incident, he'd always made it a point to say hello and pat me on the back. Naomi had told me that Trent had been acting weird, but at practice it appeared to be more than weirdness. It seemed that I was watching him become unhinged.

I hoped he didn't suspect me of being madly in love with his girlfriend.

I hoped his bad mood was the result of something entirely unrelated to me.

We ended the practice with six suicides.

Trent came in first every time, as usual. The only thing that was abnormal about it was that he ran those suicides like a man possessed. Back in the locker room, as I laced up my Chuck Taylor's and pulled on my backpack, I noticed that Trent hadn't changed with everyone else.

I walked back through the gym and saw Trent doing push-ups in the far corner. He was grunting like Rocky Balboa and interrupting him didn't seem like the brightest idea.

"Hey, Paco," he said in between heavy breaths.

"Are you doing okay?" I asked.

"Yeah, just focused," he said.

"Focused on what?"

"Beating the shit out of some punk."

"Who?" I said, scared for my life.

Trent stood up, breathing heavily and sweating profusely. His chest heaved and his muscles looked bigger than usual.

"If I tell you," he looked around the empty gym, "You have to promise not to say a word."

"I'm pretty good at keeping secrets," I reminded him.

"Yeah, you are."

Trent glanced toward the locker room doors and lowered his voice.

"You know Octavius?" Trent asked.

"The black guy?" I said. There were only three black students in the entire school.

"Yeah, him," Trent said, "I'm gonna' kick his ass after school tomorrow."

"Really? Why?"

"He's been talking a lot of smack about me," Trent said, "—and Naomi."

"Oh..." I said.

I didn't want to pry if it was about him and Naomi—that was dangerous territory to tread on.

"Octavius has been calling Naomi a slut," Trent divulged, "And he called me a 'racist nigger lover' on FriendMe last night."

I didn't know what to say to that, partially because I wasn't sure I'd heard it right. *A racist nigger lover? Wasn't that an oxymoron? It didn't make any sense. How could you be racist and love black people at the same time? And wasn't it more racist of Octavius to call Naomi a "nigger" than for Trent to be in a relationship with her?*

"—And he said that we haven't ever had sex," Trent added, "Because she'd never go for a 'white boy' like me. Can you believe that, Paco?"

So this was what Trent's weirdness and racial questions and insecurity were all about.

"No," I said, "That's pretty stupid."

It was a hard job sometimes—trying to pretend that I didn't know certain things.

"Yeah," Trent said, scanning the room again to make sure nobody else was around. "Octavius is the one who's a nigger."

Up until that point in my life, I'd only heard the word "nigger" in some movies and hip-hop songs—never out of the mouth of someone live, in-person, someone I knew, someone white and my classmate.

Not only did it sound wrong and hateful—it sounded flat out dumb. As if the whole of Western Civilization had just taken one gigantic step backward. As if everything I'd learned in school about Martin Luther King's dreams coming true were complete bullshit.

If you were there you might've thought we were in Little Rock, Arkansas, in the 1950s.

Nope. It was March 8th, 2004.

And it was the last day I considered Trent Oden anything remotely close to a friend.

THE FIGHT

About the day of the fight...

I wasn't the only one who knew Trent's plan. By lunchtime, he'd told his whole entourage, in case he needed some back up.

Of course, he'd told Naomi. He'd framed the fight as a battle to prove his love and devotion to her, to prove that racial barriers could be transcended. He said he was protecting her honor, but he was really fighting to protect his own reputation and boost his faltering ego.

Naomi knew the truth, too. She warned Trent against fighting Octavius, calling it "idiotic and immature." She said that she wouldn't watch them fight, but Trent wasn't hearing any of it.

Although I wanted to join Naomi in boycotting the brawl, some combination of odd curiosity and boy instinct pulled me toward the scene.

At 3:31, I walked behind the science building where there was a wide strip of dirt between the school's boundary fence and the building. There were about twenty students lingering there, speculating in hushed tones, waiting to see the action. Octavius was already there with a scowl on his face, his eyes focused on the door Trent would be opening at any moment. Octavius was short and stocky. Though Trent was taller, Octavius was thick and powerfully built. And he had the advantage of having nothing to lose. Trent had been placed on a pedestal. Octavius was the underdog and there must have been people in his corner. Anything could happen.

I considered the shame of Trent being a no-show. But just as that thought crossed my mind, Trent threw open the back door, trailed by his four closest friends. As if orchestrated, Trent and Octavius were soon toe to toe, waiting for someone to make the first move.

Octavius started the smack talking: "Had to bring your white-boy-crew to back you up, huh?"

"That's your problem, man," said Trent, "Everything's about race."

"Everything's about race," Octavius mocked him with an exaggerated, nasally, white-boy voice.

"You're the one who called me a nigger lover!" Trent said.

"What? What'd you just say?" Octavius raged at the sound of the word "nigger" coming from Trent's mouth. "I didn't say that, but I'm still gonna' kick your racist, punk ass!"

"I'm not racist," Trent's voice cracked. "My girlfriend is black."

"Duh, Sherlock," Octavius shot back. "I don't care if yo' grand mama's black as night. That don't mean jack."

Trent stood there like he didn't know what to say, then muttered, "You're an idiot."

"You're the one who got nothin' to say," Octavius replied.

They went back and forth with their stupid pre-fight jabber until Octavius jolted his head forward to make Trent flinch. It worked.

Trent craned his head back, then Octavius announced to everyone, "See. He scared."

It was enough to dig sharply into Trent's ego. He pushed Octavius first.

It wasn't just a push. It was a violent, unmistakable, point-of-no-return, fight-initiating thrust with two hands. The crowd let out an anxious noise that must have been how ancient Romans had reacted to the first move of the gladiators. The big push had separated them. Trent hopped nervously like a boxer while Octavius stood still, crouched and ready. With the noise that the spectators had let out, the fight was sure to be broken up in less than a minute. And it almost seemed as if Trent was waiting for that teacher-rescue because, Octavius was right, he looked frightened. *The mighty Trent was scared!*

Octavius sensed it, too, and he was getting impatient. He hadn't come for a pushing match.

"Come on, punk!" he yelled.

Taking the bait, Trent led with a weak, fake left jab and then took a big swing with his right—but the swing was too big and too slow. Octavius ducked, which sent Trent's right hand sailing over his head. Lightning quick, Octavius responded with a solid right jab that caught Trent—

defenseless with his whiffed arm across his chest—almost square on the chin. Trent's head buckled but his feet stayed in place. It was brutal. Time froze. Trent was stunned.

Neither of them moved and the crowd stood silent.

Blood started dripping, then pouring down Trent's chin.

The teenage spectators gasped at the sight of Trent's mortality.

Octavius's one punch had sent Trent's lower bicuspid through the skin right below his bottom lip. Blood oozed out of the tooth-sized hole in Trent's face and poured from his mouth as soon as he opened it up a crack.

Impressively, Trent didn't even stagger. He just stood there in disbelief. His eyes wide and watery, he looked at the blood on his hand as if he were about to die. Maybe part of him did die, right then and there.

Two teachers and a security guard showed up seconds later and all the kids, including Octavius, scattered like swatted flies. Trent remained standing in the exact same spot. He held his hand over his mouth, staring at the pool of blood forming on the light gray cement beneath him.

I was the last spectator to leave the scene, alone.

I don't think Trent realized that I'd stayed there for a few more seconds than everyone else. It was a sad sight, but in a way, he deserved it.

Trent had clearly lost the fight and was about to lose a lot more.

KARMA

As much as I wanted Naomi to dump Trent and come running into my arms, it was actually difficult to watch the unraveling of Trent Oden. After all, he had been the god of the 8th grade and had recently been somewhat nice to me—and he had something to do with my own personal renaissance. Wishing bad times upon him—anyone— would surely mean bad karma for me in the future.

I didn't want that.

The only thing I wanted was Naomi.

Was that wrong?

That night, I was on FriendMe checking the photos of all my new "friends." I revisited Naomi's pictures and, just as I was beginning to feel like a stalker, I noticed something significant. The pictures of her and Trent— once featured so prominently in her most recent album— were all gone.

I clicked on her homepage to check her status. Where there had been a painfully clear line that said "In a relationship with Trent Oden" there was nothing. *Nothing*!

In a rush of perhaps foolish joy, I messaged her. Here's what we wrote:

Paco: *How's it goin'?*

Naomi: *OK. Did you watch that idiotic fight between Mercutio and...?*

Paco: *Yes. I did... Nice allusion to Shakespeare.*

Naomi: *Thanks. And nice use of the word "allusion." Well, I know Trent lost, but even before the fight, I knew it was over.*

Paco: *Over?*

Naomi: *Our relationship. I broke up with him today. He's too immature and simple-minded and self-centered and—you know, a typical boy.*

Paco: *Oh. I'm sorry to hear that.*

Naomi: *It's a good thing. I'd been detaching myself from him for a few weeks, so I don't feel so bad about it at the moment.*

Paco: *He's probably crushed.*

Naomi: *Yeah. Probably. But it's his ego more than his heart. He'll get over it.*

Paco: *Maybe in a few years. I know if you dumped me, it would take me years, maybe decades, to recover.*

Naomi: *Come on, Paco!... You're so sweet.*

Paco: *Thanks... but I wasn't joking.*

Naomi: *By the way, I wasn't including you on the stereotypical dumb boy list.*

Paco: *Muchas gracias.*

Naomi: *De nada. What are you listening to right now?*

Paco: *Believe it or not, the Beatles.*

Naomi: *Wow, me too! "White Album"?*

Paco: *Yeah!*

Naomi: *Let me guess: You're listening to your favorite song?*
Paco: *Nope, but I will.*
Naomi: *Ha. I will too! ;)*

We continued our back and forth chat. It often came back to the Beatles and Shakespeare then returned to a random, flowing conversation. That night I slept soundly and dreamed of driving along the coast in a red convertible with Naomi smiling and laughing next to me in the passenger seat. In the dream, she was clearly in love with me. I was in love with her. Then the car sprouted wings and flew—floated—over the beach and along the coastline.

It was pure bliss.

THE GAME

The Friday after the fight was the night of the last basketball game of the season.

Because I was one of the worst players on the team and I had been on restriction, I hadn't played a single minute in any of the seven games the team had played. So it was the last game of the season, but it was the first game of my season—of my life!

True: I had never played a single minute of an organized basketball game in my life. Sure, I had played a few times at recess, during PE class, and some scrimmages in practice, but this Friday night game was the real deal—the championship game.

Before arriving at the gym that night, I wasn't nervous because I never expected to play. But once I entered the gym—the same gym where the Famous Tequila Incident had happened—and saw the bleachers pulled down and half full of spectators thirty minutes before game time, I felt butterflies crawl through my stomach.

The pre-game locker room setting didn't ease my anxiety. Trent sat silently with a big bandage across his chin.

"Hey, Paco," he mumbled and winced in pain.

"Hey, man," I said. "Are you gonna play tonight?"

He looked sad. Defeated. I didn't know what else to say to the guy. I kind of felt sorry for him. I'd lost respect for him—oh, and I desperately wanted to marry the girl who had just dumped him. So it was a bit awkward.

"I'm gonna try to play," Trent managed to say without moving his mouth much. "I have five stitches under here." He pointed to his bandage.

I knew better than to mention anything about Naomi.

I looked around the locker room and noticed only five other players.

"Where's the rest of the team?" I asked.

"Three guys—Scott, Ryan, and Todd—can't play. They're ineligible. Remember?" Trent struggled to enunciate. His words were unclear and jumbled. Whether it was more about the physical or emotional pain, I couldn't possibly know. All I knew was that it hurt to hear him speak—especially because of what he had just said.

"So there's only two subs?" I said, somewhat panicked. "Me and Eddie?"

"Eh," Trent uttered. It meant "yeah."

Coach Huskie entered the room in his shiny, game day, full blue sweat suit. It said "Walden Cougars" across the front in bright gold letters.

"Paco, you better tie those laces up tight," coach told me. "Looks like you might get some PT tonight."

Coach sighed and turned to the rest of the team with the seriousness of a commander about to lead his unit into battle.

"It's game time, gentleman."

Our significantly reduced team stood up and followed him out to the court.

On the way out I asked Eddie: "Hey, what does PT stand for?"

"Playing time," he said and shook his head.

Those words hit me hard as I followed my teammates into the bright, bustling, packed gym. I had never seen so many people in our school gym before. There must have been hundreds. Maybe even a thousand.

Damn.

...

I distinctly remember three things during the first half of that championship game:

    1) Trent's meltdown

    2) My defense of Naomi's butt cheeks

    3) My one and only shot

I suppose because of Trent's fight injury—for which nobody except Octavius was punished—our team and the coach weren't expecting much from Trent that night. But I doubt any one expected what actually happened.

It started with his first five shots. All of them were misses—bad misses. All but one of his attempts hit the rim. The crowd would have certainly chanted "air-ball" on most of his shots if it hadn't been our home crowd.

To make it worse, Trent started committing some obvious fouls against the other team.

The first two weren't bad, but the third and fourth were brutal. On the third, Trent pulled down a rebound, hunched over, and threw his elbows wildly as if he were being attacked by a pack of wild dogs. One of his elbows caught the tallest guy on the other team right in the balls! The six-foot-four kid doubled over in agony the instant Trent nailed him in the family jewels.

The crowd let out a variety of noises. The women gasped. The men groaned in shared pain.

Coach Huskie yelled at Trent and called him over to the sideline.

While Coach gave Trent a pep talk that only he could hear, Trent's chest heaved and his eyes watered. It was clear that Trent was frustrated and taking out his anger on the opposing team.

Evidently, Coach Huskie's pep talk didn't work.

On the next trip down the court, Trent dribbled hard to the basket and plowed through two defenders, knocking both to the ground. One of the opposing players fell straight backward and hit his head on the gym floor. It made a big thud.

Gasps and other concerned noises emerged from the crowd.

The referee blew the whistle. He'd had enough. He called a technical foul, which meant that Trent had fouled out of the game with one minute left in the first half. When Trent realized that he'd just eliminated himself from the game—from his middle school basketball career—he yelled in agony and plunked himself down on the middle of the court.

He pounded the gym floor with his right fist and screamed like a banshee.

Then he started crying hysterically.

All the screws holding Trent Oden together came undone right there on the gym floor in front of no less than 600 people.

It took a few minutes for the coach and the referees to pull him off the court.

The game was stopped for ten minutes.

It was a sad sight.

But what happened during that game delay was much more memorable.

While Trent was being escorted out of the gym and into the locker room, our cheerleaders did one of their routines to fill the transition time.

Naomi was one of the cheerleaders, god bless her soul. She wasn't a regular on the cheer squad—and she was the opposite of a typical cheerleader type—but she was there that night. Of course, Naomi looked amazing in her uniform: bright blue and gold.

Naomi, from the toes up:

    -White Keds.

    -Short blue cheerleader skirt.

    -Tight, sleeveless cheerleader top.

    -Golden brown arms.

-Pom-poms in both hands.

-Glowing, glittering, smiling face.

-Magical, twinkling eyes.

While the cheerleaders were on the court, my focus was dedicated to her and only her. Surprisingly, Naomi returned my attention. At one moment, when she was facing our side of the gym, she grinned and winked at me. I looked over my shoulder to see if there was some hunk of a guy standing behind me, but there was no one. Then all the cheerleaders did an about-face so that all our team and our side of the gym could see was their backsides.

For this segment of their routine Naomi climbed onto the top of the cheerleader's human pyramid. Five girls formed the base, two girls on the second story and Naomi on the top. On her way up to the top, I caught a glimpse of her butt—or at least that defining crease that separates the leg from the butt cheek. I was shocked to see that she wasn't wearing the short spandex shorts that all the cheerleaders were required to wear underneath their skirts. She must have forgotten because she was wearing normal black underwear!

So when she made it to the top of the human pyramid, I was at the perfect angle to see almost exactly what Naomi's butt looked like. I sat on that team bench gazing at her, mesmerized in my own perverted world until I realized I wasn't the only one. The entire basketball team was gawking.

"Daaaang!" Eddie said at the end of the bench, "Check out Naomi's butt."

His words hit me like a punch to the gut. In fact, they pissed me off. I turned to Eddie and blurted out, "Shut up, man!"

It just came out without thinking.

"What's your problem, Paco?" Eddie said, keeping his eyes up on Naomi.

I stood up and got right in front of him, blocking his view on purpose.

"What the hell, dude?" he protested and tried to shove me aside. I didn't budge or say a word. "What—you think Naomi's your girlfriend or something?" he asked.

"No," I said.

"Then what the hell's your problem?"

"She's a..." I started and paused because I knew that whatever came out my mouth would be laughed at or met with some form of teenage jock stupidity. But I continued, "She's a person, not a sexual object."

Eddie laughed along with most others on the bench.

"You gotta be kidding," he said to me. "What are you, gay?"

That got a few laughs too.

Usually I'm not so quick with responses, but in that moment I was.

"So, Eddie," I said, "You're saying that if I have some respect for a girl, then that makes me gay?"

"Probably," he said.

I looked back in Naomi's direction. She had just dismounted and the cheerleading team was skipping off the court.

"What if that was your mom or your sister?" I said to Eddie and, unintentionally, the whole bench of players.

"You wanna fight right here, Paco?" Eddie said and stood up.

With a newly found courage that had been absent my entire first semester at Walden, I stood my ground and said, "Why don't you stare at your mom or your sister's butt, Eddie?"

"You really want to die now, huh?"

Eddie balled his hands into fists.

"It's not because you're gay," I said. "It's because you respect them and you don't see them as sexual objects."

Eddie didn't have a comeback. Neither did any of the players on the bench. I balled my hands into fists and Eddie knew he had to say something so he started with "Who the hell do you—" but Coach interrupted him.

"Sit down and shut up!" Coach Huskie barked as he returned to the bench.

While Coach talked to the team, I was still lost in my confrontation with Eddie. I had been ready to fight for Naomi—not as an object or possession—but as a human being who I deeply cared for. Yes, I'd been staring at her butt too, but there were deep feelings connected to my staring. It was as if my words to Eddie and the team were coming from another person within me who was directing the message at a slightly younger, dumber version of me: "*Paco, respect Naomi. Don't view her as a sexual object. You are in love with her.*" And love gave me courage. In fact, my almost-fight-with-Eddie may have been my first outward act of true love.

Coach Huskie's intense and thunderous voice snapped me out of my introspection.

"Paco!" he yelled. "You're in!"

What?!

Remember: I had never played in a real game and this was the championship game. There was a minute left in the half and the opposing team—the Jackson Jaguars—was winning by three points.

Coach Huskie had us in a huddle and told us quite a few things very quickly. Half of it sounded strategic and the other half purely inspirational, but I didn't understand a word of it. Honestly, he might as well have been speaking Chinese. I was nervous, clueless, and still thinking about Naomi.

When the whistle blew, Coach Huskie patted me on the back and said, "Do the right thing, Paco."

The right thing? How was I supposed to know what that was?

During my first fifty-five seconds in the game, it was as if I was on a basketball court for the first time ever—as if I'd momentarily forgotten all the rules of the game. I found myself simply running back and forth across the court whenever it seemed that everyone on my team was running in one direction. In the last seconds of the half, I took the same cues from the opposing players and began running back toward the basket where our team was shooting (I knew that much, at least). That's when Alan Jacobsen passed me the ball. As soon as I caught it, I heard the distinct sound of my coach and the entire gym counting down: "4, 3, 2..."

Coach yelled at the top of his lungs, "Shoot!"

So I shot the ball—a massive heave from half court.

Miraculously, it went in. A swish right at the buzzer!

My team and half of the gym jumped out of their seats.

Coach Huskie and my teammates—except for Eddie— hugged me. It was great, but undeserved. It was pure luck, but totally awesome.

You know what the best part was?

As our team trotted back to the locker rooms, Naomi gave me a big, passionate, sweet smelling hug and called me a "stud."

...

The second half was a blur.

I stayed on the court the rest of the game, just trying to keep up with the guy I was guarding and not make any glaring mistakes. Alan Jacobsen filled in the gap left by Trent's absence and did most of the scoring. His shooting kept us in the game, but just barely. Jackson maintained a two or three point lead on us. I concentrated on sticking to my man, playing the best defense I could. Luckily, I was guarding what seemed like the worst player on the other team. He was chubby, slow, and reeked like a homeless man.

Because the game was so intense and I was actually playing for once, I lost track of Naomi. The crowd was all wound up. They reacted to every pass, rebound, and shot—make or miss. And then, as if I were in a time warp, there were only thirty seconds left in the game.

That's when Alan hit a three pointer to put our team up by one point. The crowd erupted as if it were an NBA game and they all had a lot of money riding on the winner. It was crazy how vocal the parents were getting. Because scoring was slow in middle school games (the score was 35-34) Alan's shot seemed to clinch the win for us. But Jackson wasn't going down that easily. They inbounded the ball, raced down the court, and scored on a driving lay-up that put them up again by one point.

There were 10 seconds left on the clock.

Jackson pressured us with tough defense as soon as we put the ball in play. They wanted to make us panic, force us to make an error, or at least make it difficult to get a clean shot off.

Why or how I got the ball passed to me is still a mystery, but as soon as I got it I raced toward our basket. Because the guy who was guarding me was slow, I made it past him and appeared to have a clear lane to the basket.

But I didn't.

My easy lay up turned into an easy block for the big guy on the other team. Luckily, it was a block and a foul. He had fouled me in the act of shooting.

So there I was at the free throw line—a place I had never been before—with two seconds left. I could make one shot and tie the game. Make two and win the game. Or miss both and single-handedly lose the game.

Coach Huskie called a timeout.

In the huddle he told us, "If Paco misses these shots, you need to foul your man immediately. If he makes one, then make sure you don't foul!" Coach paused, made sure to look every player in the eye, then looked directly at me. "But you don't have to worry about any of that, because Paco is going to make both of his free throws, right, Paco?"

I could have said "No," or "Maybe," or "I'll try my best," but I didn't. I just nodded my head and really believed I'd make those shots.

And, miracle of miracles, I did!

I made both shots with everyone watching—including Naomi who stood right next to the basket with the other cheerleaders. In fact, in between my two shots, after I made the first one, Naomi winked at me—again.

Jackson didn't even get a shot off in the last two seconds and we won the championship game!

Some people said that I won the championship game, even though I scored a measly five points. Whenever people told me such congratulatory nonsense I either told them that Alan was the real hero (he scored 22 points) or I told them that I got lucky.

Both answers were true.

I was just happy that I didn't screw up.

More importantly, I was happy that Naomi had winked at me.

Twice.

And I was ready to fight for her.

UNDER THE BLESSED MOON

I left the gym that night on a natural high.

Everyone had something nice to say to me, including Naomi.

"You're amazing, Paco," she said and gave me a big hug. Did she really say that? Did she hug me so passionately on purpose? What did it all mean? It was like a dream.

My dad drove me home—he had been in the stands and I didn't even know it. He was beside himself with pride in my performance, which was kind of silly. Why was it that adults operated like this? I could have done some brave humanitarian act earlier in the day, but I was getting all the praise in the world for putting an inflated ball into a metal hoop.

Regardless, it was nice to get all the positive attention.

If I were an NBA player, I suppose the team would have gone out and celebrated at a high profile club. We'd signs autographs and take pictures. We'd get VIP treatment.

But we were all in 8th grade so after our brief locker room celebration, our parents drove us home. Trent's parents must have driven him home—or to a psych ward—before the game had ended because he was nowhere to be found after the final buzzer.

Back at home, my dad explained to my mom how it had been a great game and how I'd been the hero, but she just nodded in approval, unable to visualize all the sport-lingo details my dad laid out. Still, she seemed proud. She gave me a big hug and kiss on the cheek and wished me a good night.

"You make sure to take a shower before bed, mijo!" she said. "Buenas noches."

And that's how it seemed my glorious night would end—with a shower, laying down in bed, and falling asleep.

And that's almost what happened.

But seconds after I lay down in bed, I heard a light knocking on my window.

...

Shocked, I cautiously approached my window and cracked the shutters to see outside. It was Naomi! *How did she get to my house? How the hell had she found my house? How did she know which window was mine?*

I opened the window and said hello.

"Hi Paco," she said. "I hope you don't mind me knocking on your bedroom window."

"Yes," I said, "I mean, 'No' I don't mind. You can come over anytime."

"You were so awesome tonight," she said.

"I was lucky."

"Yeah, maybe it's your lucky night," she said.

"What do you mean?" I said.

I didn't really have my wits about me because Naomi was talking to me through my bedroom window and I was in my pajamas, which was almost too much to handle.

"Can you jump down here?" she asked.

"Yeah, but we have to whisper," I said. "I don't want my parents to—"

"Gotcha," she said at a lower volume.

I didn't bother to put pants or shoes on. I climbed up on the windowsill and jumped six feet down to the cold grass. It was a good thing my house was only one story, because if Naomi had summoned me from a second or third floor building, I still would have jumped.

She was that phenomenal.

And, on that night, she was particularly forward with me.

"Paco," she said, "Why do you reference the song 'I Will' with me so much?"

"Because I like it?" I said, oddly ending the last syllable with a question mark.

"Not because it says 'Who knows how much I love you?'" she asked, point blank.

"Yeah," I said. "You got me."

"'You got me?' That's not very romantic, Paco," she said, clearly disappointed.

At that moment something came over me. Clearly, Naomi had come to my house at 11pm on a Friday night for a reason—risking a lot just to see me. She didn't want another hug, or to congratulate me for a good game. She was free from Trent and interested in me. Why else would she appear outside my window late at night?

So I would waste no more time. I wanted to kiss her and I had to try. I had nothing to lose.

I counted down in my head.

10, 9, 8, 7...

"Paco, are you okay?" she asked.

"Yeah, I'm just counting down silently," I said, as if it were perfectly normal.

3, 2...

"Paco, wha—"

And that's when I kissed her.

Yes, I interrupted her with a kiss. Her lips had just parted to make the "a" sound in the word "what." Our lips locked and my hands wrapped around the small of her back.

A few seconds into it, she slipped her tongue gently into my mouth and I followed her lead. Naomi ran her fingers through my hair, which multiplied the tingly, goose-bumpy sensations that overtook my body. We stood there and held each other and kissed for a long, long time without ever pulling way.

Five minutes straight, maybe ten?

How to describe that kiss? Heaven on earth? Bliss? Nirvana? These words don't seem sufficient.

"Oh my god, Paco," she said. "That was the best kiss ever."

"That was my first kiss ever," I said.

"Well, you're a natural."

I didn't know what to say. I'd just kissed the girl of my dreams and she seemed to enjoy it as much as I did. Part of me wanted to ask her to marry me right then and there, but I didn't want to freak her out. The other part of me wanted to just keep kissing her for the rest of the night. I no longer cared if my parents caught and punished me. This was worth years of being in a solitary jail cell. I was ready to sacrifice for her. I was ready to be with Naomi in whatever way possible—even if we had to wait a while, or keep it secret from Trent. I was ready. I didn't want to get too far ahead of myself, but I was ready to—

"Paco," Naomi cut off my blissful train of thought. "I'm sorry."

"Sorry for what?" I asked. "You just gave me the best moment of my life."

"That was pretty amazing," she said. "But your life has just begun. So—

"So let's..." I barely stopped myself from finishing that phrase with "get married." I was so smitten, I could've said many ridiculous things. That's why I paused. After an awkward silence, I said, "Let's be together, Naomi."

Hallelujah! Yes, let's be together! Damn, I said it.

Naomi took a step back and I could see her demeanor shift. Her face wore an expression that said she had to tell me something that I might not want to hear. No—something that I definitely didn't want to hear.

"That's a nice idea, a great idea—but there's a slight problem," Naomi said.

"What, that we're young and dumb?" I said defensively, "Like Romeo and Juliet?"

"We're not like them," she said. "They end up dying."

"Okay, then..."

"For the record," Naomi said, "Romeo and Juliet was the best love story ever."

"Why, because it was short?" I said. "Two days. Is that what you're getting at?"

Naomi took a small step back, distancing herself from me only a few inches, and it struck me with a heavy feeling—the kind where your heart and insides feel like they're about to be yanked out from underneath you.

"No, because Shakespeare told the truth," she said.

"And what's that?" I asked.

"Love is painful. Love is tragic," she said. "And sometimes love is momentary."

Why are you ruining this already, Naomi? Why are you being so cynical? I wanted to protest loudly but all I could do was give her a perplexed look.

"I have to go," she said, then she winked and smiled at me, and her eyes sparkled again. It brought back that rush-of-love-feeling.

"I have to go," she repeated, "...to Bulgaria."

What? Was she joking? Bulgaria?!

"Uh, are you kidding?" I said with a nervous laugh.

"No," she said. "It may sound crazy, but my dad was transferred. He starts his new job at the US embassy in Sofia, Bulgaria on Monday. We leave tomorrow night. I know it's weird and totally out of the blue and the timing is bad, but I have no choice, Paco."

I was speechless inside and out.

Naomi continued, "In some ways it's good. I'll start fresh. I'll be in a new place, a new school, far away from this mess Trent created."

Naomi went on explaining, holding my hands, trying to make it all sound less horrible than it really was. For me it was like a great dream that had quickly turned into a nightmare. A sinking feeling pulled down on me, as if gravitational forces had just tripled. Disbelief. Denial—the desire to fight and sacrifice and do whatever I had to in order to keep Naomi from moving away. *But what could I do? What would a modern Romeo have done? Juliette? Wait—they would have killed themselves!*

"I don't know what to say," I said. I felt the cold grass underneath my feet. My toes were freezing. I looked up at the moon. It was full. It didn't seem real.

Life didn't seem real.

"You don't have to say anything," Naomi said. "Just don't be mad at me. It's not my fault."

"I know," I said, still looking at the moon, crushed.

"I'll miss you, Paco Jones," she said, as a tear streaked down her left cheek.

"Will I ever see you again?" I asked, and it clicked—our Beatles song. "Will I have to wait a lonely lifetime?"

"If you want me to, I will," she responded, without skipping a beat.

I kept it going: "Well, I guess 'It doesn't really matter... I will always feel the same.'"

It may have been a bit cheesy, but it seemed the best way to express my love for her without actually saying "I love you" and then bursting into tears.

"At when at last you find me," she said, switching the pronouns around, "Our song will fill the air..."

"I'm gonna remember you said that," I told her, stopping the song game. "I promise."

She smiled and kissed me on the cheek. "Can you promise me something else, Paco?"

"Sure."

"Promise you won't hate me," she said. "But don't love me either, okay?"

"I could never hate you. You saved me," I said.

"Saved you?"

"Yeah," I said. "When I met you I was Paco-Taco, or whatever, with bird crap smeared all over my face. Honestly, I was about to give up—to accept being the poor, loser Mexican kid who flunked out. Failed. But you were kind to me. You gave me hope. You gave me something to dream about. Something to fight for."

"Something?" Naomi asked.

"Love," I said without my usual hesitation.

"Love?"

"Yes, and you—whether you loved me back or not—taught me what love really is. It's not about your beautiful face or sweet smile or perfect body. While all that stuff is a nice bonus, it's really about how you understood my embarrassment in the bathroom. That first time we talked about Romeo and Juliet, talked on the phone about the Beatles *White Album*, connected to each other by criticizing the gossipers, the weird racism, and the general ridiculousness of our middle school."

Naomi's watery eyes were locked on mine as I spoke. Now *she* was the speechless one.

"We just kissed, and that was awesome, but all I really want is to be around you, close to you. The feeling you give me just from a few words or a smile—it's magical. It's not normal. Like tonight at the game, it's a long story, but I was ready to fight for you and I can't fight at all. I'd probably get killed in a fight—torn to pieces. But I'm pretty sure that it was love that made me feel invincible. It was my caring for you, Naomi, that gave me the courage, the confidence I'd never had before. It's probably why I made those shots and the reason you're standing in front of me right now. So as much as you're breaking my heart by leaving, I can really only thank you...Thank you, Naomi."

At this, Naomi cried and gave me a huge hug.

The power of her embrace confused my mind and emotions. Feeling her body so tightly pressed against mine, the fruity smell of her hair, the gentle breath she let out so close to my ear—all were good things. Great things. But the reason she was pressed against me was not good. It was the worst. It was goodbye—from the highest high to the lowest low. After the long hug, she took a few quick steps backward.

"I love you, Paco Jones," she said, with tears in her eyes.

Naomi turned around and ran down the moonlit sidewalk without looking back.

That was the last time I saw her, under the blessed moon.

It was also the last time I've been so in love.

BLUE MONDAY

That Monday at school was empty without Naomi—especially when I was in Mr. Holliday's class, staring at her vacant seat. I was lost in memories of her when Trent walked into class late. His body language and entire "look" told the story of a broken soul. He was dressed as if he'd grabbed dirty clothes off his bedroom floor and threw them on. His disheveled hair was greasy and his puffy red eyes were sunken, with dark circles. It looked like he hadn't eaten or slept for days. Making it even worse, his bandage was off and his stitched, discolored chin was exposed.

Mr. Holliday began the class by silently taking attendance, glancing up and down the rows without saying a word. When he was finished with his task, he stood up from his computer.

"Good morning, class," he said.

The class's response was a mumbled, indifferent scattering of "Good mornings."

"I have some sad news," he announced, "Naomi Fox will no longer be gracing us with her presence...I was told that she's moving to Bulgaria—of all places—with her family. I don't know if she told any of her classmates, but this news came as a surprise to all of her teachers. It meant that we never had the chance to say goodbye to her."

Mr. Holliday said those last few words as if he were giving a eulogy, his eyes cast on the desk of Trent Oden.

Trent's head was straight down, dejected. Mr. Holliday probably didn't want to pour salt on Trent's wounds by asking him to sit up straight.

A few minutes later, while we were doing our writing warm up, Trent excused himself to go to the bathroom.

I couldn't bring myself to write anything on the blank page that morning. I was still shell-shocked. Naomi had crushed both Trent and I in the course of a few days. She was a powerful girl. Who knew what carnage, what path of broken hearts, she'd leave in Bulgaria.

Where was Bulgaria, anyways?

I opened my geography book, searched for Bulgaria, and found it above Greece, below Romania, west of the Black Sea. I wondered what the color of the Black Sea was. Black? Blue? Green? Then I practiced my alliteration just to write something down—anything to distract me.

-Black Sea.

-Bulgaria

-Broken hearts

-Broken dreams

-Bathroom

Bathroom?

Trent had been in the bathroom for a while and it began to worry me. If I was depressed at the loss of Naomi after one kiss, I couldn't fathom what Trent was going through. He'd been with her all year, and he'd just lost a fight, a game, and his pride—everything!

Though I didn't consider myself his friend, I couldn't help but empathize with Trent's depressed state. *Was he really in the bathroom—or was he running away from school, on his way to the nearest bridge or tall building? Was he the type who'd commit suicide? I would have never considered it, but after the last week, who knew? Was he as vulnerable, insecure, and fragile as Naomi had said?* As our silent writing time dragged on, I couldn't get the idea of Trent committing suicide out of my head. Call it instinct—or intuition.

In a polite, hushed voice, I asked Mr. Holliday if I could go to the bathroom.

"You know my bathroom policy, Paco," he said. "One at a time."

"I know, Mr. Holliday," I said, "But this is really an emergency."

I cringed and held my hands near my pelvis to indicate that I was in pain. I usually wasn't a good actor, but this performance was solid.

"Huh," Mr. Holliday grunted. "Okay, Paco. Hurry up."

I speed-walked out of the room and ran to the nearest bathroom.

Trent wasn't there.

I ran upstairs to the only other bathroom in the building. There were two lanky seventh graders in a stall smoking a cigarette.

"Have you guys seen Trent Oden?" I asked. I was on a mission.

"No, man," one kid said, "Hey, don't rat on us."

I shook my head and ran out.

I jogged down the hall without knowing where I was going. Where could he be?

If he was off-campus, it was already too late. He could be anywhere. But the security guards wouldn't have let a kid run out during school hours in broad daylight. How could I spot him? The roof?

The roof!

The building was only three stories tall, but Trent was not of sound mind and anything was possible. I took the not-so-secret-stairwell to the top. If I was caught on the roof and Trent wasn't up there, I'd be in clear violation of my probation. I could be expelled from school for ditching class and being in a restricted area. But this might be life or death.

I nudged open the door and felt brisk, fresh air.

"Trent?" I said, looking around. "Trent?"

"Paco?" I heard him say, but couldn't see him.

I moved across the flat part of the roof and walked up to the knee-high curb where the burnt orange Spanish tiles began and sloped steeply down to the roof's edge.

I saw Trent there, sitting precariously close to the edge.

"Trent, have you lost your mind?" I said.

"I've pretty much lost everything, Paco," he said.

"Dude, you're only fourteen!" I said. "Your life hasn't even really started yet."

"Maybe for you," he said, "I can't even imagine..."

Trent must have gone off on another line of thought too depressing to voice out loud.

"You know what she wrote to me last night?" he asked me.

"What?" I said, feeling halfway guilty for having—if for only an instant—taken Naomi from him. But my guilt was only half-baked because I hadn't "taken" her at all. She'd left him—left both of us.

"I wrote her a long message about how destroyed I've been since she dumped me," he said.

"...And?"

"And she told me not to feel too bad about it because it wasn't my fault... She explained that she is probably a *lesbian* because she is attracted to girls, too! And she thinks a relationship with a girl will be safer and more emotionally rewarding, or whatever."

"Lesbian?" I said, shocked. My jaw dropped. It didn't make any sense.

"Yeah, bro," Trent said, "That's why I can't deal with this—with this life. I just want to end it."

"Are you kidding, Trent?" I said. "Because you got dumped, you're gonna kill yourself? That's just dumb. You're smarter than that. You're better than that. Everybody goes through tough times."

I sounded like a second-rate middle school counselor.

"I thought Naomi loved me," Trent said. "But I'm so lame I turned her into a *lesbian*!"

"Why are you saying 'lesbian' like that? I asked.

"Like what?"

"I don't know. Like it's a disease," I said.

"Oh, yeah. My bad," he said.

"—Trent, did it ever cross your mind that she might just be trying to ease your pain by putting the blame on herself rather than anything you did? You know, she's that smart, Trent. Like a psychologist."

Trent's expression indicated that he hadn't considered that option at all. I had just made up the faux-lesbian theory on the spot, but it seemed possible that Naomi might make up such a thing in order to spare Trent—and protect me. She was *that* smart. At any rate, it had backfired.

"Now, please, crawl back up here before you do something you'll regret," I said. "Plus, that drop isn't high enough to kill you anyway."

"You wanna bet?" he said.

"No, I don't."

Trent peeked over the edge from his sitting position. He looked back at me. Fear gripped his eyes.

"Maybe, you're right, Paco," he said. "Maybe Naomi was just saying that to make me feel better."

"Forget about her," I said, though I couldn't imagine ever forgetting about Naomi Fox.

"Is life supposed to suck this much?" Trent asked, as if I suddenly had all the answers.

"I don't know... Sometimes?" I noticed his hand shaking. "The thing is, she's gone, Trent. She's on a different continent now, and we can't do anything about it."

"And...?"

"You have to move on. Remember all the great things about her and move on."

"That sucks," he said.

"Yeah, it sucks big time," I said, and something about the situation made us both laugh.

"Promise not to tell anyone about this?" he pleaded. Turned out, that was his one condition for not committing suicide that day. He didn't want his middle school peers to know. Life and death teetered on the gossipy opinion of his peers. Ridiculous.

"I promise," I said.

Trent twisted his body so that his shoulders faced me at the center of the roof. He used his right foot to boost himself up the slope, but the tile cracked and slipped out from under his shoe. He was lying flat, face down, the soles of his designer shoes near the ledge. Trent's hands gripped the tiles in a panic. He looked up at me in terror.

"Shit!" he yelled. "Help me, Paco!"

Damn. I couldn't do much to help him. I didn't have a rope. There was nothing around me to throw to him. If I walked out onto the tiles it would just make it worse—more broken, unstable terracotta and not one but two teenage boys falling off the roof and dying during Mr. Holliday's class.

I grabbed the corner and reached my left hand out toward Trent, but he would have to make it a good ten feet before I could grab his hand.

Trent tried to crawl up the sloping roof. His first effort got him about a foot closer to me and away from the edge. But his second effort failed miserably. Two tiles broke under his feet and the one under his right hand slid off completely. As the tiles cracked and slid down, so did Trent.

Frozen in place, I watched his panicked body slide off of the roof and disappear.

He screamed all the way down.

Then there was a blunt thud.

THE END

Trent Oden didn't die that day.

Thankfully, the three-story building proved an inadequate height for suicide.

He ended up hitting a tree branch on the way down, landing feet-first on the grass, and badly breaking both legs and one wrist, which put him in a wheelchair for the rest of the semester. Because he missed so much class time and was an emotional wreck, he failed most of his classes.

If one had a dark sense of humor, they might say that Trent Oden failed at just about everything that semester— including killing himself.

But, as I and only a few others know, he had changed his mind at the last minute. He wasn't attempting to commit suicide. It was just an embarrassing accident—an epic fail, if you will.

That's what Dr. Bennett, in more eloquent words, delivered as the official report at our somber school-wide assembly the next day. The official non-suicide report was the result of a meeting between me, Mr. Holliday, and Dr. Bennett.

Since I was the only witness to this near-tragic incident, my testimony was very heavily relied on. I told them the entire story of that morning—from lying about needing to go pee to hearing the surprisingly quiet sound of Trent hitting the ground.

Mr. Holliday and Dr. Bennett nodded and listened.

When I was finished, Dr. Bennett told us that a suicide attempt—even an accidental one—would create bad press for the school. He used the word "liability" a lot. Even the mention of the word "suicide," he explained, would lower enrollment and generally freak everyone out. They'd call in the evening news, psychologists, and suicide prevention groups. The school would be put on watch for years and Mr. Holliday would be considered negligent. Dr. Bennett sounded more like a clever lawyer than a middle school principal. Better to call it an embarrassing accident by a truant, irresponsible teenager, he said, and leave it at that.

Dr. Bennett spoke with Trent and he agreed to stick to the irresponsible freak accident story.

It was also in Trent's interest to call it a dumb accident while ditching class rather than a "failed suicide attempt," especially considering his other recent failures.

And so it went.

For my cooperation and honest reporting, I was thanked, officially cleared of my probationary status, and offered a partial scholarship for the remainder of the year—on the condition that I never said a word about the meeting in Dr. Bennett's office.

Politics 101.

Mr. Holliday and I walked out of the principal's office together that day.

He turned to me in the hallway with a suspicious grin. "There's much more to the story than that, isn't there, Paco?"

I returned his grin and exercised my right to remain silent.

"You know," he said, "You should write about it some day."

I immediately thought of Naomi.

"Who knows?" I said. "Maybe *I will.*"

Dominic Carrillo is a writer and teacher from San Diego, California. He is a regular contributor to the *San Diego Reader* and is the author of *To Be Frank Diego*, a novel, and *Americano Abroad*, a travel memoir. *The Improbable Rise of Paco Jones* is his first YA novel.

TEACHER'S GUIDE

Common Core Aligned Questions

Reading

CCSS.ELA-LITERACY.RL.8.1: Cite the textual evidence that most strongly supports an analysis of what the text says explicitly as well as inferences drawn from the text.

- What does the text say explicitly about Paco's self-esteem or identity in the beginning of the story?
- What inference can you make about Trent's group of friends? What specific evidence supports your inference?
- What inference can you make about Naomi or Paco's perspective on middle school? What specific evidence supports your inference?

CCSS.ELA-LITERACY.RL.8.2: Determine a theme or central idea of a text and analyze its development over the course of the text, including its relationship to the characters, setting, and plot.

- How does the theme of "the difficulty of young love" develop over the course of the novel?
- How does the theme of "struggling with one's identity" develop throughout the novel?
- What other central idea can be found in this story? (What evidence supports your claim?)

- How does the author use the setting at Walden Academy to develop the themes?

CCSS.ELA-LITERACY.RL.8.3: Analyze how particular lines of dialogue or incidents in a story propel the action, reveal aspects of a character, or provoke a decision.

- What particular lines in the story lead to the fight between Trent and Octavius?
- Which lines of dialogue reveal that Paco feels alienated or does not fit in?
- How does the dialogue between Paco and Naomi foreshadow Trent's meltdown?

CCSS.ELA-LITERACY.RL.8.4: Determine the meaning of words and phrases as they are used in a text, including figurative and connotative meanings; analyze the impact of specific word choices on meaning and tone, including analogies or allusions to other texts.

- What are three examples of the author using figurative language? What does each example mean in the context of the story? Does it provide imagery for the reader?
- What are the connotative meanings of the following words: radiant, ominous, articulate, monotone, lout, sigh, slut?
- What specific words had an impact on the meaning or tone of a scene in the story?

- Which allusions did you connect with? (Shakespeare, the Beatles, Cyrano, *Dia de Los Muertos*, Rocky, etc.) Did they enhance or distract from the meaning of the text? Why?

CCSS.ELA-LITERACY.RL.8.6: Analyze how differences in the points of view of the characters and the audience or reader create such effects as humor.

- How do the differences in Paco and Mr Holiday's points of view create humor?
- Is the irony of Trent's situation in the second to last chapter humorous or tragic? Why? What evidence supports your claim?

CCSS.ELA-LITERACY.RL.8.9: Analyze how a modern work of fiction draws on themes, patterns of events, or character types from myths, traditional stories, or religious works such as the Bible, including describing how the material is rendered new.

- How does the theme of young love mirror other stories, yet have an original twist?
- Do story events—such as Paco reading the private note, Paco ghost writing for Trent, or the basketball game—draw on classic stories or myths? How?
- How does Paco's character draw on other classic character types? What makes him unique?

- How is Naomi's character both familiar and original?

Writing

CCSS.ELA-LITERACY.W.8.1: Write arguments to support claims with relevant evidence.

- Make a claim about one of Paco's character traits in the first half of the novel. Support that claim with specific evidence from the text.
- Make a claim about one of Mr Holiday's character traits during "The Dance" chapter. Support that claim with specific evidence from the text.
- Make a claim about one of Naomi's character traits based on the "Under the Blessed Moon" chapter. Support that claim with specific evidence.

CCSS.ELA-LITERACY.W.8.2: Write explanatory texts to examine a topic and convey ideas, concepts, and information through the selection, organization, and analysis of relevant content.

- In chronological order, write the three main events that led to Paco's rise in self-esteem.
- Write about the character Nicol. Why was she in the story? What idea or concept did she represent?

CCSS.ELA-LITERACY.W.8.3: *Write narratives to develop real or imagined experiences or events using effective technique, relevant descriptive details, and well-structured event sequences.*

- Paco does not tell much about his old school, Dolores. Using a similar style to the author, write a short story that describes a scene that Paco was involved in at his old school.

- Naomi exits the story somewhat abruptly. Write a diary entry or letter, from her point of view, addressed to Paco weeks after her departure.

- Mr Holiday seems to be an observant secondary character—someone who has witnessed a lot of the story himself. Re-write any scene from the story, but from his perspective.

CPSIA information can be obtained
at www.ICGtesting.com
Printed in the USA
LVOW04s1006080516

487239LV00021B/919/P